Life in the Country

Life in the Country

Giovanni Verga

Translated by J. G. Nichols

ET REMOTISSIMA PROPE

100 PAGES

100 PAGES

Published by Hesperus Press Limited

4 Rickett Street, London sw6 1ru

www.hesperuspress.com

First published in Italian in 1880

This translation first published by Hesperus Press Limited, 2003

Introduction and English language translation © J.G. Nichols, 2003

Foreword © Paul Bailey, 2003

isbn: 1-84391-042-x

CONTENTS

FOREWORD

Giovanni Verga was on the brink of middle age when he transformed himself into one of the world's greatest storytellers. He was already a writer of popular fiction, with plots that flirted with easy melodrama. He was a familiar figure in the artistic and literary salons of Florence and Milan. But then he changed course by returning to his native Sicily – in spirit to begin with, subsequently in the flesh – and to the region of Catania, under the shadow of Mount Etna, in particular. The wonderful tales in this book appeared in 1880, and they remain as fresh, as real, and as profoundly engaging as when they were written.

They exemplify – the best of them – storytelling of the purest kind. The reader is allowed to be the freest of free agents, since there is no attempt on Verga's part to manipulate or control his or her feelings. The people who engage his disinterested attention are vividly realised, with an intensity that comes from deep knowledge of their centuries-old way of life. They are poor, mostly, these fated men and women, toiling beneath a pitiless sun for the little money the rich landowners and the feared and miserly middlemen are prepared to pay them. The likes of Foxfur, in 'Nasty Foxfur', and Jeli – the heroic victim of circumstance in the masterpiece 'Jeli the Herdboy' – grab at happiness when and where they can, and face disaster with something akin to stoicism, because their reasons for carrying on are neither spelt out nor explained. I find Verga's writing bracingly pessimistic, its undertones of comedy and light-heartedness in exquisite contrast to the inevitable tragedy that occurs in the closing paragraphs. The tragic events are described without relish, almost matter-of-factly. Verga never indulges in the luxury of psychology, in the manner of those nineteenth-century novelists who worry away at their characters' motives for doing even the simplest things. With severe artistic reserve, and acute narrative judgement, he sets down what happens, and in his hands it is always enough.

In the story 'Bindweed's Lover' which is addressed and dedicated to his friend, the now-forgotten novelist Salvatore Farina, Verga accounts for his new-found purpose as a narrator. He wants the hand of the artist to 'be absolutely invisible' and the work of art to 'seem to have been made by itself'. The novel or story will be a 'natural occurrence', every element in it growing 'spontaneously'. This was revolutionary thinking in the prevailing Italian culture of his day, and it cannot be said to be fashionable at present. The author who insists on occupying the narrative, however modestly, is still the safest bet for the average reader, who craves explanation and explication. When Verga turned his back on the novels and plays that brought him early success, his reputation suffered as a result. The swooning, hothouse prose of Gabriele D'Annunzio and others became anathema to him. His favoured austerity, which so disconcerted his contemporaries, is now – in the eyes and ears of admirers such as myself – his most formidable strength.

Anyone coming to the story 'Rustic Honour' ('*Cavalleria rusticana*') after long exposure to Pietro Mascagni's opera of the same name, will be shocked and surprised. The opera, for all its virtues, is a sentimental concoction. Mascagni's score is musical treacle, smothering each of Verga's protagonists in ever larger dollops of glucose. The opera is based on Verga's own adaptation for the stage, in which the jealous and vengeful Santa became Santuzza, a role he expanded for Eleonora Duse, whose genius was celebrated by Bernard

Shaw and discredited by Max Beerbohm. Verga loathed what Mascagni and his librettist did to the bleak little story and there were years of legal wranglings over unpaid royalties, amongst other complications. The original endures as a landmark in the history of storytelling. Turiddu, Lola, Santa and Alfio are afforded only a few lines of dialogue and their characters are sketched in, but every word is apropos. And Verga is nowhere to be seen.

He is similarly absent from 'She-Wolf', which he also adapted for the theatre. (Anna Magnani triumphed in the title part in Rome in the 1950s.) Stories don't come more basic than this one, which tells of a woman's all-pervading lust for her son-in-law Nanni, who has a single, terrible means of escaping from her. This is another of Verga's magisterial sketches, displaying a profound awareness of the vagaries of human behaviour in a matter of pages. Again, there is no elaboration for elaboration's sake – just the desolate tale itself, unadorned.

Yet Verga is a consummate stylist. He seldom resorts to Sicilian dialect, and on the rare occasions he does so it is invariably to encapsulate something peculiar to the island. He captures the essence of lives unafflicted by the demands of intellect and in which the common passions and needs are constantly to the fore. These are lives, too, that were plagued by superstition and an unforgiving brand of Catholicism, with women being the principal cause of sin and transgression. No one inhabits the simple mind better than Giovanni Verga, who refuses either to ennoble or to sentimentalise the peasants he gives such immediate literary life. His humane genius is at its most telling, in every sense, in the awesome 'Nasty Foxfur' ('*Rosso Malpelo*'). The eponymous subject of this study in quotidian cruelty is given a nickname – Malpelo literally means 'evil hair' – because red hair was associated with the devil's offspring. The boy's father dies in a sand mine, and the lonely, despised youth befriends another ugly boy, called Frog. Foxfur beats and abuses Frog, to teach him how to survive in a vindictive society, but his lessons in survival turn out badly. Verga sends Foxfur to his awaited doom and the story ends with the reader feeling that a life has been wasted almost at its very inception. I love *Life in the Country*, for reasons to do with undemonstrative compassion and self-abnegating understanding – qualities as abiding in great art as they are sporadic in day-to-day existence.

– *Paul Bailey, 2003*

How is it that such simple stories as these can affect us so deeply? Typically, a series of events is outlined, without much or even any elaboration, where one thing leads inexorably to another and the end result is disaster. There is usually little indication of motive, except for the most obvious indicated in the broadest of terms – *amour fou*, say, or the lust for revenge – and the characters are seen almost entirely from the outside. But character is revealed by actions, even by apparently trivial actions. In 'Jeli the Herdboy', just after the disaster which would cost Jeli his job and lead eventually to an even greater disaster, Jeli and his companion weep:

> 'The travellers who were going to the fair, when they heard that weeping in the dark, asked what they had lost. And then, once they knew, they went on their way.'

In the space of a few words we, the readers, move from assuming on the part of the travellers a desire to help to the realisation that they are just curious. Verga does not himself draw out these implications: it is so much more effective to leave that to us. The author does not need to emphasise his point because, we sense, that is simply how things are. A little later in the same story Jeli is left alone, with the dead horse in the ravine by the side of the road:

> 'The steward and Alfio went away, with the other colts which did not even stop to see where Star was left, and as they went they tugged at the grass along the side of the road.'

The horses are not even curious. But we are aware here, not so much of the intellectual superiority of the human beings, as of their being part of the same environment as the horses, with the same needs. Verga's art is, then, an art of implication. And a too-rapid reading may easily miss some of the implications. Who, for instance, gets the most satisfactory revenge in 'Rustic Honour'?

Verga's procedures are poles apart from those of many novelists. Much of his art consists in what is not said. He avoids the procedures of depth psychology which were being developed by others as he wrote, and which, in only a few years, were to reach a climax in the work of Freud. Depth psychology is by its very nature endless in scope: its *raison d'être* is that there is always something more to reveal, since the human onion has so many skins. It might seem that Verga's method would, by contrast, be inevitably very limited in scope. In these stories it may be limited, but it is not too limited. The method can be seen at its best in 'Nasty Foxfur'. Foxfur is thought by everyone – his mother, his sister, his workmates, himself, and at times it seems, by the author – to be evil. He is not, but this fact is not revealed by a glorious act of unselfishness, say, but by the implications of his very ordinary actions and his apparently simple thoughts. How his surroundings have helped to make him what he is implied, for instance, when we are told that he could not understand why Frog's mother should weep for the death of her son, when that son cost more than he was worth to keep. Even more strikingly, we get a notion of the goodness of Foxfur from a repulsive action of his – his beating of poor Frog, the cripple!

'At times he beat him without cause and without mercy, and if Frog did not defend himself, he beat him harder, and more furiously, and said to him, "Take that, jackass! A jackass is what you are! If you haven't got the guts to defend yourself against someone who doesn't even hate you, it means that you'll let every Tom, Dick, and Harry walk all over you!"'

He is cruel, but cruel to be kind, for Frog has something to learn and Foxfur is trying to teach him. And it is not only the chief characters in the stories whose complexity is revealed. It is noticeable, for instance, what a clear, and rounded, notion we have even of Farmer Agrippino when we come to the end of 'Jeli the Herdboy'.

It is a pity that Verga did not always leave his artistic intentions to be understood by their results. The contrast between society life and peasant life which is at the heart of the first piece, 'A Reverie', is not the best thing in the book. This is because Verga is not here content to present, but feels he needs to argue. There is even at times a touch of sentimentality:

'You, as you clasp your blue-fox muff to your chest, will be happy to recall that you once gave the poor old man a little money.'

This first piece is more of a thesis than a story. While there is no doubt that 'The War of the Saints' is a story, and a good one, it is a touch patronising occasionally, provoking the reaction that these are 'funny little peasants'. It is significant that it is the only story in this collection which ends with a moral being drawn, although admittedly the author does not do this *in propria persona*. Usually Verga has little overt interest in morals, in any sense of that word. Such minor lapses do serve to throw into relief Verga's customary invulnerability to such objections. Verga's voice is distinctive and readily recognised, but it defies parody. Objectivity and restraint are hard to imitate, let alone to mock, and Verga's dependence on the reader's ability to draw conclusions is perceived as a compliment, and does not provoke any urge to mock.

This is perhaps surprising because the actions and reactions of the protagonists in these stories are often so very extreme. The eponymous protagonists of 'She-Wolf' and 'Bindweed's Lover' are the victims, and the destructive agents, not so much of *amour fou* as of a love which is downright crazy. And yet they are truly frightening, and not in the least ridiculous. This is largely the result of the stark presentation of actions with little or no comment. We see by example what Verga meant when he hoped for stories in the future in which 'the hand of the artist will be absolutely invisible, and the novel will bear the stamp of a real happening, and the work of art will seem to have been made by itself.'

– *J.G. Nichols, 2003*

Note on the Text:
This translation is based on the edition: *Verga. Tutte le Novelle*, Mondadori (Oscar Classici), Milan, 1983, vol. 1.

Life in the Country

A Reverie

Once, when the train was passing near Aci-Trezza, you went to the window of the carriage and exclaimed: 'I'd like to spend a month down there!'

We went back, and we spent, not a month there, but forty-eight hours. The locals, who stared with wide-open eyes when they saw your huge amount of luggage, must have believed that we were going to stay there for a couple of years. On the morning of the third day, tired of seeing the same everlasting green and blue and of counting the carts that went along the road, you were on the station, fiddling with the chain of your scent-bottle, and craning your neck to catch sight of the train which seemed as if it would never come. In those forty-eight hours we did everything which could be done in Aci-Trezza. We walked along the dusty road, and we clambered on the rocks. Pretending to learn to row, you got blisters on your hands inside their gloves, which cried out to be kissed. We spent a very romantic night on the sea, casting the nets chiefly in order to do something which would look to the boatmen as though it was worth catching rheumatism for. And dawn surprised us on the height of the rocky stack, a pale unpretentious dawn, which I can still see now, streaked with broad violet reflections, on a dark green sea. It was curled like a caress around that little group of hovels which slept huddled on the shore. And, on the very top of the cliff, against the depths of a transparent sky, your tiny figure stood out clearly – the outline which you owed to your skilful dressmaker, and the fine and elegant profile which was yours alone. You wore a lovely grey dress which seemed designed to match the colours of the dawn. A beautiful picture indeed! And one could guess that you thought that too, from the way in which you posed in your shawl, your large weary eyes smiling at that strange spectacle, and also at the strangeness of finding yourself present at it. What came into your dear mind while you were contemplating the rising sun? Were you perhaps asking him in what other hemisphere he would find you one month hence? But you merely said ingenuously: 'I don't understand how anyone could live here all his life.'

And yet, look, that is easier to do than it might seem. All that you need first of all is not to have an income of a hundred thousand lire. And then, in compensation, to suffer a few of all the hardships there are among those gigantic rocks, set in azure, which made you clap your hands in admiration. That is all it takes for those poor devils, who dozed while they waited for us in the boat, to find in their picturesque ramshackle hovels (which, seen from a distance, looked to you as though they too must be seasick) all that you try so hard to find in Paris, in Nice, in Naples.

It is a strange thing. But perhaps it is not a bad thing that it should be so – for you, and for all the others like you. That heap of hovels is inhabited by fishermen. 'Seafolk' they call themselves, as someone else might say 'gentlefolk'. Their skin is harder than the bread they eat, when they do eat, since the sea is not always kind, as it was when it kissed your gloves… On its bad days, when it rumbles and snorts, there is nothing to be done but stand and look at it from the shore, or stretch out flat on the face, which is better for anyone who has not eaten. On those days the entrance to the inn is crowded, but few coins rattle on the tin counter, and the urchins who grow abundantly in the village (as if poverty were a good compost) scream and squabble as if they had the devil in them.

4

Every now and then typhoid, cholera, bad times, gales come and sweep away all that swarm who, you might imagine, would like nothing better than to be swept away and disappear. And yet it always forms again in the same place. I cannot say how or why.

Have you ever happened to find yourself, after a shower of rain in the autumn, putting to rout an army of ants by idly tracing the name of your last dancing-partner on the sand in the avenue? Some of those wretched little creatures will stay stuck to the ferrule of your parasol, twisting and writhing. But all the others, after five minutes of panic-stricken dashing about, will go back and cling desperately to their little brown mound. You would certainly never return there, and neither would I. But in order to comprehend such stubbornness, which is in some ways heroic, we too have to become tiny, we have to narrow the whole horizon to the space between two clods of earth, and look through a microscope at the little reasons why little hearts beat. Would you too like to put your eyes to that lens, you who look at life through the other end of the telescope? The spectacle will look strange to you, and for that reason will perhaps amuse you.

We have been very friendly. Do you remember? And you asked me to dedicate some pages to you. Why? *à quoi bon?* as you tend to say. What can be the value of anything I write to anyone who knows you? And what are you to anyone who does not know you? Nevertheless, I recalled that whim of yours one day when I saw again that poor woman to whom you used to give charity under the pretence of buying her oranges which were laid out in a row on a little bench outside her door. Now the bench is no longer there, they have cut down the medlar tree in the yard, and the house has a new window.[1] Only the woman herself has not changed. She was rather more to one side, holding out her hand to the carters, and crouching on the little heap of stones which barricades the old national guard post. And I, as I strolled around with a cigar in my mouth, thought that even she, poor as she is, had seen you pass by, pale and proud.

Do not be angry that I was reminded of you in such a way and in connection with such a subject. Apart from the happy memories you have left me with, I have a hundred others, vague, confused, disparate, collected here and there, I no longer know where. Some of them perhaps are memories of daydreams, and in the confusion which they brought about in my mind, while I was going down that little lane where so many sad and happy things have gone on, the cape of that poor shivering woman, as she crouched there, made me feel sad and made me think of you, glutted with everything, even with the adulation which the fashionable papers throw at your feet, often quoting you at the head of their column of society news – so glutted as to think up the whim of seeing your name in the pages of a book.

When I come to write the book, you may not be thinking of it any more. Nevertheless, the memories I send you, so distant to you in all senses of the word, to you intoxicated with feasts and flowers, will give you the sensation of a delicious breeze in the sultry nights of your everlasting carnival. On the day when you return down south, if indeed you do return, and we sit side by side once more, kicking the stones with our feet, and kicking fancies with our thoughts, we may perhaps talk about those other intoxications which life has elsewhere. You may even imagine that my mind dwells on that forgotten corner of the world either because you have set foot in it, or to distract my mind from the glitter which follows you everywhere – whether the glitter of jewels or of fever – or even because I have looked for you in vain in all those places which rejoice in being fashionable. You can see from this that you always take pride of place, whether here or in the theatre.

Do you remember also that old man who took the helm of our boat? You do owe him that debt of gratitude because he so often kept you from soaking your lovely light blue stockings. He is dead now, over in the city hospital, the poor devil, in a great white ward, between white sheets, chewing white bread, cared for by the white hands of the Sisters of Charity, whose only fault was that they could not understand the pitiful wailing of the poor man, mumbling in his semi-barbarous dialect.

But if he had been allowed to have any wishes, he would have wanted to die in that dark corner by the fire, where his palliasse had lain for so many years, 'under his own roof'. He wanted this so much that when they carried him away he wept and whimpered as old people do. He had always lived within those four walls, facing that beautiful and treacherous sea, which he had to struggle with every day, both to get a living out of it and to avoid leaving his bones there. And yet in those moments when he was quietly enjoying his 'bit of sunlight', crouching on the foot-rest of his boat, with his arms round his knees, he would not have turned his head to look at you, and you would have searched in vain in those dull eyes of his for any reflection of your beauty in its greatest pride. Not like those occasions when haughty heads bow low and line the way to let you pass between, in resplendent salons, and you are mirrored in the envious eyes of your best friends!

Life is rich, as you can see, and full of inexhaustible variety, and in your own way you can enjoy, without any qualms, that portion of wealth which has fallen to your lot. That girl, for instance, who was peeping out from behind the pots of basil,

7

when the rustle of your dress caused a commotion in the lane, if she caught sight of another well-known face at the window opposite, smiled just as though she too were dressed in silk. Who knows what poor joys she was dreaming of, leaning on her window-sill, behind that sweet-scented basil, with her eyes fixed on that other house covered with vine-shoots? And the smile in her eyes would not have ended in bitter tears, up there, in the big city, far from the stones which had known her from her birth, if her grandfather had not died in hospital, and her father had not drowned, and her whole family had not been scattered by one gust of wind which blew on them – a fatal gust of wind which transported one of her brothers even into one of the prisons of Pantelleria, 'in trouble', as they say down there.

Theirs was a happier fate who died: one of them, the biggest, at Lissa, he who looked to you like a bronze David, standing upright with his harpoon in his fist, and lit up suddenly by the flames of the blazing ivy-torch.[2] Big and strong as he was, even he flushed bright red if you fixed your ardent eyes upon his face. Nevertheless, he died like a good sailor, on the spar of the foremast, standing firm next to the shrouds, lifting his cap in the air, and saluting the colours for the last time with his wild manly islander's shout. The other one – that man who on the islet did not dare touch your foot to free it from the rabbit-snare in which you had got it entangled, scatterbrained as you are – he was lost on a dark winter night, among the billows when, between his boat and the shore – where his people were waiting for him, running to and fro like madmen – there were seventy miles of darkness and storm. You could not have imagined what desperate and gloomy courage that man was capable of in his fight against death, he who had allowed himself to be intimidated by the masterwork of your shoemaker.

It is better for them who have died and do not 'eat the king's bread'[3] (like that poor chap who has stayed on Pantelleria) or that other bread which his sister eats, and do not go about as the woman with her oranges does, living on what God sends, which in Aci-Trezza is very little. The dead at least do not lack for anything! The landlady's son said the same thing, the last time he went to the hospital to ask after the old man, and to take him in secret some of those stuffed snails which are so nice to suck for anyone who has no teeth left. He found the bed empty, with the covers nice and straight, and he slunk into the courtyard and placed himself in front of a door covered with old scraps of paper, and peered through the keyhole at a great empty hall, cold and echoing even in summer, and saw the end of a long marble table, over which a sheet was thrown, heavy and stiff. And he said that the people in there at least did not lack for anything any more, and, to while away the time, he started to suck the snails one by one, since they were no longer any use. You, as you clasp your blue-fox muff to your chest, will be happy to recall that you once gave the poor old man a hundred lire.

Among those left behind are the urchins who escorted you like jackals and laid siege to the oranges. They are left behind to buzz round the beggar-woman, to fumble about in her skirts, as though she had some bread in them, to gather up cabbage-stumps, orange peel, and cigar-ends, all those things which are dropped on the road, but which must preserve some value, since there are poor people who survive on them. In fact the poor people live so well on them that those plump, hungry little ragamuffins will grow up in the mud and dust of the roadway, and will become big and strong like their fathers and their grandfathers, and they will populate Aci-Trezza with more little ragamuffins, who will happily hang onto life by the

9

skin of their teeth as long as they can, like the old grandfather, without wanting anything else. And if they do want to do anything different from what he did, that will be to close their eyes where they opened them, cared for by the village doctor who comes every day on his donkey, like Jesus Christ, to help the good people who are leaving this life.

'In short, the oyster's ideal way to live!' you will say.

Precisely, the oyster's ideal way to live, and the only reason why we find it ridiculous is that we ourselves were not born oysters. Besides, this tenacious attachment of these poor people to the rock onto which Fate has let them fall (while it was scattering princes and duchesses here and there), this brave resignation to a life of hardship, this religion of the family, which is reflected in their work, in their houses, and in the stones which surround their houses, seems to me – for a quarter of an hour anyway – something which is very serious and worthy of great respect. It seems to me that a restless, wandering mind would fall asleep peacefully in the serenity of those mild, simple feelings which continue calm and un-changed from generation to generation. It even seems to me that I could watch you pass by – your horses trotting briskly, with their harness jingling cheerfully – and in all tranquillity salute you.

It is perhaps because I have tried too hard to see into the hustle and bustle which surrounds you and follows you that I now think that I can discern a fatal necessity in the tenacious affections of the weak, in the instinct which makes little people cling together to resist life's storms. And so I have tried to decipher the humble and obscure drama which must defeat the plebeian actors whom we both once knew. This is a drama which I shall perhaps recount to you sometimes, a drama whose core seems to me to consist in this: when one of those little creatures, either weaker, or less cautious, or more egoistic than the others, tries to detach himself from the group, enticed by the unknown, or driven by an urge to better himself, or out of sheer curiosity about the world – then the world, man-eating monster that it is, swallows him up, and his nearest relatives too. You can see that in this respect the drama is not without interest. For the oyster, the most interesting topic must be that which deals with the wiles of the lobster or of the diver's knife which detaches it from its rock.

Jeli the Herdboy

Jeli, who herded the horses, was thirteen when he first got to know Don Alfonso, the young squire. But he was so little that he did not reach up to the belly of Whitey, the old white mare who wore the herd's bell. He was always to be seen here and there, on the hills and on the plain, where his animals were feeding, upright and motionless on some cliff, or crouched on a big stone. His friend Don Alfonso, when he was in the country on holiday, visited him at Tebidi every single day, and shared with him his little bit of chocolate, or the herdboy's barley bread, and the fruit they stole from his neighbour. At first Jeli called the young squire 'Excellency', as they do in Sicily, but once they had come to blows good and proper, their friendship was firmly established. Jeli taught his friend how to clamber up to the magpies' nests at the top of the walnut trees which were higher than the belfry at Licodia, to hit a sparrow in flight with a stone, and to mount at one leap onto the bare backs of his half-wild horses, grabbing by its mane the first one that came within range, without being confused by the angry neighing of the unbroken colts and their desperate bucking. Ah! those wonderful gallops across the mown fields, with manes streaming in the wind! Those beautiful April days when the wind swept the green grass up into heaps, and the mares were neighing in the meadows; those beautiful summer noons, when the white countryside fell silent beneath the hazy sky, and the crickets crackled in the turf, as if the stubble were bursting into flames; the beautiful winter sky glimpsed between the bare branches of the almond trees, which were shuddering in the north wind; the frozen lane which rang beneath the horses' hooves; and the larks which sang so high above, in the heat, in the azure; the lovely summer evenings which came up very gently like mist; the pleasant scent of the hay into which you could sink your elbows; and the melancholy buzzing of the evening insects; and those two notes from Jeli's flute, always the same – yoo! yoo! reminiscent of distant things, of the feast of St John, of Christmas night, of the ringing of bells in the dawn, of all those great events of the past, which seem sad because they are so far away, and make you look up into the sky with tears in your eyes, as if all the stars brightening up above were raining down into your heart and flooding it!

Jeli, however, did not suffer from that melancholy. He was crouched on his bank, with his cheeks puffed out, intent on playing yoo! yoo! yoo! Then he mustered the herd by dint of shouts and stones, and drove them into the stable, beyond the Hill of the Cross.

Panting, he climbed the slope across the valley, shouting sometimes to his friend Alfonso, 'Call the dog! Oi! Call the dog!' Or else, 'Fling a heavy stone at that bay colt who struts like a little lord and dawdles along, stopping at every shrub in the valley.' Or else, 'Bring me a big needle tomorrow morning, one of Lia's.'

He knew how to do anything with a needle, and he had a little bunch of rags in his canvas bag, to patch his breeches or his jacket-sleeves when necessary. He could also make braids out of horsehair. And he himself washed in the clay-streams of the valley the kerchief which he wore round his neck when he was cold. In short, as long as he had his bag over his shoulder, he needed no one in the world, whether in the woods at Resecone, or lost in the centre of the plain of Caltagirone. Lia used to say, 'You see Jeli the herdboy? He's always been alone in the fields, as if his mares had dropped him, and so he

13

can make the sign of the cross with both hands!'

But, although it is true that Jeli had no need of anyone, those who worked at the farm would have been happy to do anything for him, since he was a helpful boy, and it was always possible to get something in return from him. Lia baked his bread out of sheer love for her neighbour, and he repaid her with nice wicker egg-baskets, cane wool-winders, and other little things. 'We're like his horses,' said Lia, 'that scratch each other's backs.'

At Tebidi everyone knew him from when he was so little that he could not be seen among the horses' tails, when they were grazing on the Plain of the Stretcher-bearer, and you could say that he had grown up under their eyes, although no one ever saw him, and he was always wandering here and there with his herd. 'He fell from heaven like rain, and the earth took him up,' as the proverb says. He really was one of those who have no home or parents. His mother was in service at Vizzini, and she only saw him once a year when he went with the colts to the fair of St John. And the day she died, they came to fetch him one Saturday evening, and on the Monday Jeli returned to his herd, so that the peasant who had taken his place in charge of the herd would not lose one day's work. But the poor boy had come back so upset that once or twice he let the colts run into the crops. 'Hey, Jeli!' Farmer Agrippino shouted at him from the farmyard. 'Do you want a real taste of my whip, you son of a bitch?' Jeli set off at a run after the scattered colts, and drove them dispiritedly towards the hill. But his mother was always in his mind, her head wrapped in a white kerchief, and not speaking to him any more.

His father was a cowherd at Ragoleti, beyond Licodia, 'where there is so much malaria that you could reap it', as the peasants round about said. But in malarial lands the grass is good, and cows do not catch fever. So Jeli stayed in the fields the whole year round, either at Don Ferrante, or in the Commenda fields, or in the Jacitano Valley, and the huntsmen or the travellers who took the short cuts used to see him here and there, like a dog without a master. He did not mind, because he was used to being with his horses which went in front of him, step by step, browsing on the clover, and with the birds which wandered about around him in flocks, all the time the sun was making its very slow journey, until the shadows lengthened and then disappeared. He had the time to see the clouds gather together little by little and to imagine mountains and valleys in them. He knew how the wind blows when a storm is brewing, and what colour the clouds are when it is about to snow. Everything had its own appearance and its own meaning, and there was always something to see and something to hear every hour of the day. And so towards evening, when the herdboy started playing on his elderwood flute, the black mare approached, chewing the clover listlessly, and she remained looking at him with her large, thoughtful eyes.

The only place where he did suffer from a touch of melancholy was on the bare moors of Passanitello, where no bushes or shrubs rise up, and in the hot months no birds fly. The horses gathered in a circle, with their heads drooping, to provide some shade for each other, and on those long days when the threshing was taking place that great silent light rained down uninterruptedly for sixteen hours.

Where the pasturage was abundant, however, and the horses were glad to linger, the boy occupied himself with other things. He made cane cages for crickets, carved tobacco-pipes, and rush baskets. With four small branches he could erect some sort of shelter when the north wind was driving the crows in long files through the valley, or when the cicadas were beating their wings in the sun which was burning the stubble. He roasted acorns from the oak-wood on the embers of sumac branches, which was like eating roast chestnuts, or he toasted bread in large slices in the same way, when it was getting bearded with mould, because when he was at Passanitello in the winter, the roads were so bad that sometimes he went a fortnight without seeing a living soul go by.

Don Alfonso, whose parents wrapped him in cotton wool, envied his friend Jeli his canvas bag in which he kept all his goods – bread, onions, the flask of wine, the kerchief for the cold, the bundle of rags with the big needles and thread, the tin box with its flint and tinder. He also envied him the superb grey-black mare, that animal with a tuft of hair standing up on her forehead, who had wicked eyes, and whose nostrils swelled like those of a snarling mastiff when anyone attempted to mount her. She did however let Jeli mount her and scratch her ears, which she would not let anyone else do, and she used to go sniffing round to hear what he had to say. 'Don't mess with the grey-black mare,' Jeli advised him. 'She isn't wicked, but she doesn't know you.'

After Scordu, the man from Buccheri, had led away the Calabrian mare which he had bought at the fair of St John, on the understanding that she was to be kept in the herd until the grape-harvest, the unspotted colt, now left an orphan, was restless, but roved about on the hilltops, continually neighing in lament, and with its nostrils distended in the wind. Jeli ran behind it, calling after it loudly, and the colt paused to listen, with its neck stretched out and its ears twitching, lashing its flanks with its tail. 'It's because they've taken his mother away, and he doesn't know what to do,' observed the herdboy. 'Now I must keep my eye on him, because he might let himself fall

16

off the cliff. I remember when my mother died, I couldn't see out of my eyes.'

Then, after the colt had started to smell the clover, and take a few unwilling bites: 'Look! He's beginning to forget it gradually.'

'But he will be sold too. Horses are there to be sold, just as lambs are born to go to the slaughter, and the clouds bring rain. Only the birds have nothing to do but sing and fly all day long.'

His ideas did not come to him clearly and in order, one after the other, for he had seldom had anyone to talk to, and so he was in no rush to unearth his ideas and disentangle them in the back of his mind, where he was accustomed to let them appear and sprout little by little, like buds on branches in the sun. 'Even the birds,' he added, 'have to earn their food, and when snow covers the ground they die.'

Then he thought about it for a while. 'You're like the birds, except that when winter comes you can stay by the fire doing nothing.'

But Don Alfonso replied that he too had to go to school and learn. Then Jeli opened his eyes wide, and was all ears when the young squire began to read, and looked suspiciously at his book and him, staying to listen with that slight blinking of the eyes which signifies intense attention in those animals which are most like men. He liked poetry, which caressed his ears with the harmony of an incomprehensible song, and at times he wrinkled his brow and lifted his chin, and there appeared to be something going on inside him. Then he nodded again and again in agreement, with a cunning smile, and he scratched his head. Then when the young squire started to write, to show all the things he could do, Jeli could have stood for days on end watching him, but all at once he let a suspicious glance escape him. He could not be persuaded that you could repeat on paper those words he had said, or which Don Alfonso had said, and even what had never come out of his mouth, and so he ended up with that cunning smile on his face.

Every new idea that knocked to gain admittance to his head made him suspicious, and he seemed to sniff at it with the savage mistrust of his grey-black mare. However, he showed no surprise at anything at all. If they had said to him that in the cities the horses rode in carriages, he would have remained impassive, with that mask of oriental indifference which gives the Sicilian peasant his dignity. Apparently he entrenched himself instinctively in his ignorance, as if that were the strength of being poor. Any time when he could not think of an argument he repeated, 'I know nothing about it. I'm poor,' with that obstinate smile which would have liked to be cunning.

He had asked his friend Alfonso to write the name Mara for him on a scrap of paper which he had found who knows where – since he picked up everything he saw on the ground – and had put into his bundle of rags. One day, after he had been silent for a while, looking about absent-mindedly, he said very seriously:

'I have a sweetheart.'

Alfonso, even though he knew how to write, opened his eyes wide. 'Yes,' repeated Jeli, 'Mara, the daughter of Farmer Agrippino who used to be here. And now he's at Marineo, in that great building on the plain which you can see from the Plain of the Stretcher-bearer, over there.'

'You're going to get married then?'

'Yes, when I'm big and I get six onze[4] a year. Mara doesn't know anything about it yet.'

'Why haven't you told her?'

18

Jeli shook his head, and began to think. Then he unfolded his bundle of rags and spread out the piece of paper which had been written on.

'It's really true that it does say Mara. Don Gesualdo, the field-warden, read it too, and Brother Cola when he came over, looking for some beans.'

'Someone who knows how to write,' he observed then, 'is like someone who keeps words in a steel box, and he can carry them round in his pocket, and even send them here and there.'

'Now what will you do with that bit of paper, you who can't read?' Don Alfonso asked him.

Jeli shrugged his shoulders, but went on folding his written script carefully in the bundle of rags.

He had known Mara since she was a baby, and they had begun by having a good scrap, when they had met once down in the valley, collecting blackberries. The little girl, who knew she was 'on her property', had seized Jeli by the collar as a thief. For a short while they exchanged blows on the back, one for you and one for me, as the cooper does on the rings of a barrel, but when they were tired they gradually calmed down, still holding each other tight.

'Who are you?' Mara asked him.

And when Jeli, who was the wilder of the two, did not say who he was:

'I am Mara, the daughter of Farmer Agrippino, who is the field-warden of all the fields here.'

Then Jeli let his grasp slip entirely, and the little girl began to gather up the blackberries that she had let fall in the struggle, looking sidelong at her adversary from time to time, out of curiosity.

'Over the little bridge, in the garden-hedge, there are lots of big blackberries,' said the little girl, 'and the hens eat them.'

Jeli meanwhile was stealing away, and Mara, after following him with her eyes as long as she could see him in the oakwood, turned her back too, and took to her heels homewards.

But from that day onwards they grew accustomed to each other. Mara went to the parapet of the little bridge to spin her tow, and Jeli gradually drove his herd towards the slopes of Bandit's Hill. At first he stayed apart, buzzing around her, looking at her suspiciously from a distance, and little by little he came closer to her, with the cautious motion of a dog that is used to having stones thrown at it. When at long last they were by each other, they remained for long hours without opening their mouths. Jeli observed carefully the intricate work on the stockings which her mother had put round Mara's neck, while she watched him cutting fine zigzags on a stick of almondwood. Then they went away in different directions, without saying a word, and the little girl, when she came in sight of the house, started to run, making her little petticoat fly up on her red legs.

When the prickly pears were ripe they settled down in the thick of the bushes, peeling the pears the whole day long. They wandered together beneath the hundred-year-old walnut trees, and Jeli beat so many walnuts that they poured down as thick as hail. And the little girl tired herself out trying with shouts of delight to gather up more than she could. And then she was off, very quickly, holding the two corners of her apron spread out, swaying about like a little old woman.

During the winter Mara did not venture to poke her nose out of doors, the cold was so great. Sometimes, towards evening, smoke could be seen coming from the little fires of sumac wood which Jeli was lighting on the Plain of the Stretcher-bearer or on the Hill of Macca, so that he would not end up frozen stiff like those titmice which are found in the morning behind a stone or in the shelter of a clod of earth. Even the horses were glad to swing their tails about round the fire, and they kept close to each other to get warmer.

In March the larks returned to the plain, the sparrows to the roofs, the leaves and nests to the hedges, and Mara once again took to going for walks with Jeli in the soft grass, among the bushes in bloom, beneath the trees which were still bare but starting to be dotted with green. Jeli went in deep among the thorns like a bloodhound to uncover the thrushes' nests, while the birds looked at him in dismay with their little eyes like peppercorns. The two youngsters often carried inside their shirts little rabbits which had just left their lairs, and were almost without fur, but already had the long, restless ears. They raced through the fields after the herd of horses, going into the stubble behind the reapers, step by step with the herd, pausing whenever a mare stopped to rip up a mouthful of grass. In the evening, when they came to the little bridge, they went off, one this way and one the other, without saying goodbye.

The whole summer was spent in this way. Meanwhile the sun began to set behind the Hill of the Cross, and the robins went after it towards the mountains, as it grew dark, following it among the bushes of prickly pears. The crickets and cicadas could no longer be heard, and a deep melancholy spread through the air at that time of day.

This was when Jeli's father, the cowherd, came to his hovel. He had been stricken with malaria at Ragoleti and could not even hold himself upright on the donkey that brought him. Jeli very quickly lit the fire, and ran to the houses to look for some hens' eggs for him. 'Best spread a little straw by the fire,' his father said to him. 'I feel my fever coming back.'

Buried under his cloak, the donkey's saddle-bag, and Jeli's bag, Menu shuddered so much with the fever that he looked like a trembling leaf in November, in front of those blazing twigs which made his face look as white as a dead man's face. The peasants came from the farm to ask him, 'How do you feel, Menu?' The poor man's only reply was a yelp like that of a sucking puppy. 'It's the kind of malaria that kills you faster than a bullet,' said his friends, warming their hands by the fire.

They even sent for the doctor, but that was money thrown away, because the malaria was of the kind that was so well-known and obvious that a boy could have cured it. If the fever was not the kind that kills you anyway, it would be cured immediately with sulphate. Menu spent an arm and a leg buying sulphate, but it was just like throwing money down the drain. 'Take a good extract of *eucalipters* that doesn't cost anything,' suggested Farmer Agrippino, 'and if it doesn't do you any more good than the sulphate, at least you won't waste your money.' He even took a decoction of eucalyptus, but the fever always came back, stronger than ever. Jeli helped his father as well as he could. Every morning, before he went off with the colts, he left him the decoction prepared in the cup, the bundle of twigs near to hand, and the eggs in the hot cinders. Early in the evening he came back with more wood for the night and the small flask of wine and some little pieces of mutton which he had run as far as Licodia to buy. The poor boy did everything nicely, like a good housewife, and his father, following him with his tired eyes as he did little jobs here and there in the hovel, smiled from time to time, thinking that the boy would be able to look after himself when he was left alone.

On those days when the fever abated for a few hours, Menu got up, very confused, with his head wrapped in a kerchief, and went to the threshold to wait for Jeli while the sun was still hot. As Jeli let his bundle of wood fall by the side of the door and placed the flask and the eggs on the table, his father said to him, 'Put the *eucalipters* on to boil for tonight,' or else, 'Remember your Aunt Agata is looking after your mother's gold, when I'm no longer here.' Jeli nodded in understanding.

'It's no use,' repeated Farmer Agrippino every time he came home after visiting Menu in his fever. 'His blood is full of the plague.' Menu listened to him without batting an eyelid, with his face whiter than his cap.

By now he could no longer get up. Jeli began to cry when he did not have the strength to help him turn over. Gradually Menu got to the stage that he could not speak any more. The last words he said to the boy were:

'When I'm dead go to the owner of the cows at Ragoleti, and get him to give you the three onze and the twelve measures of wheat which are owing from May till now.'

'No,' replied Jeli, 'it's only two and a quarter onze, because it's more than a month since you left the cows, and we must deal fairly with the boss.'

'That's true!' affirmed Menu, half-closing his eyes.

'Now I'm really alone in the world like a lost colt, which the wolves could eat!' thought Jeli, when they had carried his father to the cemetery at Licodia.

Mara had come too, to see the dead man's house, with all the curiosity which frightening things arouse. 'You see how I'm left?' Jeli said to her, and the little girl drew back, overcome by the fear that he might make her enter the house where the dead man had been.

Jeli went to collect his father's earnings, and then he went with his herd to Passanitello, where the grass was already high on the land which had been left fallow, and the pasture was abundant. And so the colts stayed at pasture there for a long time. Meanwhile Jeli grew up. 'And Mara too must have grown,' he often thought while he was playing his flute. And when he came back to Tebidi after such a long time, driving the mares slowly before him along the slippery lanes of Uncle Cosimo's Spring, his eyes kept searching for the little bridge in the valley, and the cottage in the Jacitano Valley, and the roofs of the 'big houses' where the doves always used to flutter. But at that time the owner had sacked Farmer Agrippino and all Mara's family were moving out. Jeli found the girl, who had grown up and was now buxom, at the gate of the courtyard, keeping her eye on her things as they were loaded onto the cart. The empty room now seemed darker and more smoky than usual. The table, and the bed, and the chest of drawers, and the pictures of the Virgin and St John, and even the nails to hang the seed pumpkins on had left marks on the walls where they had been for so many years. 'We're going away,' Mara said to him when she saw him looking. 'We're going down to Marineo where there's that big building on the plain.'

Jeli threw himself into helping Farmer Agrippino and Lia load the cart, and when there was nothing left to carry out of the room, he went to sit with Mara on the edge of the drinking trough. 'Even houses,' he said to her, when he had seen the last basket piled onto the cart, 'even houses, when things have been taken out of them, don't seem the same.'

'At Marineo,' answered Mara, 'we'll have a nicer room, my mother's told me, one as big as the storeroom for the cheeses.'

'Now that you've gone, I don't want to come here any more. It'll look to me as if winter's come back, seeing that door closed.'

'But at Marineo we'll have other people – Pudda with the red hair, and the steward's daughter. We'll have a good time.

Over eighty people will come for the harvesting, there'll be a bagpipe, and there'll be dancing in the farmyard.'

Farmer Agrippino and his wife had already set off with the cart, and Mara ran after them happily, carrying the basket with the pigeons. Jeli would have liked to go with her as far as the little bridge, and when Mara was about to disappear into the valley he called out, 'Mara! Hey! Mara!'

'What do you want?' Mara asked.

He did not know what he wanted. 'And you, what are you going to do here all alone?' the girl asked him then.

'I'll stay with the colts.'

Mara skipped away, and he remained motionless, until he could hear the noise of the cart bouncing on the stones. The sun was touching the high rocks on the Hill of the Cross, the grey foliage of the olive trees vanished into the twilight, and across the vast countryside, far into the distance, nothing could be heard but Whitey's bell in the growing silence.

Mara, among fresh faces at Marineo, and with all the business of the harvest, forgot him. But Jeli was always thinking of her, because he had nothing else to do during those long days spent looking at his horses' tails. He had no reason now to slip down into the valley, beyond the little bridge, and he was seen no more at the farm. This was why it was a while before he knew that Mara was engaged to be married. A lot of water had flowed under the little bridge. He saw the girl again only on the feast of St John, when he went to the fair with colts to sell. That was a feast-day that turned to poison for him, and took the bread out of his mouth, because of an accident which happened to one of the owner's colts, Lord preserve us!

On the day of the fair the steward was waiting for the colts from dawn, walking up and down in his varnished boots behind the rumps of the horses and mules, standing in lines here and there along the main road. The fair was about to end, and Jeli had still not appeared with his animals round the bend of the road. On the parched slopes of Calvary and Windmill Hill there were still a few flocks of sheep, crowded into a circle with their muzzles to the ground and their eyes dull, and a few brace of oxen, with long hair, the sort that are sold to pay the rent for the land, waiting motionless under the blazing sun. Over there, towards the valley, the bell of St John was ringing for High Mass, accompanied by a continual crackling of firecrackers. Then the fairground seemed to jump, and a shout rang out and spread among the tents of the pedlars on Cocks' Climb, went down through the streets of the village, and seemed to return to the valley where the church was. Long live St John!

'Bloody hell!' shrieked the steward. 'That swine Jeli will make me miss the fair!'

The sheep lifted up their muzzles in astonishment, and they started to bleat as one, and even the oxen stepped forward a few paces, looking round with their large intent eyes.

The steward was in such a rage because that was the day he had to pay the rent for the big fields, 'when St John's day has dawned', as the contract said, and he had put money aside to complete the amount, relying on the sale of the colts. Meanwhile it seemed as if all the colts, horses, and mules that the Lord had ever made were there, all groomed and shiny, and decorated with bows, pompons, and bells, swishing their tails to drive away the boredom, and turning their heads to everyone who passed, and looking as if they were just waiting for some kind soul to buy them.

'He'll have fallen asleep, that wretch!' the steward went on shouting. 'And he's leaving me with the colts on my hands.'

Jeli had on the contrary been walking all night so that the colts would be fresh when they arrived at the fair, and would be able to get a good place when they arrived, and he had reached Crow's Plain when the Three Kings[5] had still not set, but were shining over Mount Arthur, with their arms folded. Carts and people on horseback were continually passing along the road, going to the fair. For this reason the youth kept his eyes wide open, so that the colts, frightened by the unaccustomed coming and going, should not scatter but go together along the side of the road, behind Whitey who was walking straight ahead peacefully, with the bell round her neck. From time to time, when the road came to the top of a hill, the bell of St John could be heard in the distance, so that even in the dark and silence of the countryside the feast-day could be sensed. And the whole way along the main road, far in the distance, and wherever there were people on foot or on horseback going to Vizzini they could be heard shouting, 'Long live St John!' And rockets were shooting straight up, shining behind the hills of Canziria, like the shooting stars in August.

'It's like Christmas night!' Jeli kept saying to the boy who was helping him to drive the herd. 'In all the farms there are celebrations and illuminations, and you can see fires everywhere throughout the countryside.'

The boy was dozing, putting one foot slowly in front of the other, and he did not answer. But Jeli, who felt his blood stirred by the sound of that bell, could not keep quiet. It was as if each of those rockets which slipped and shone silently across the darkness was springing from his soul.

'Mara will be at the fair of St John too,' he said, 'because she goes every year.'

And without being troubled by the fact that the boy, Alfio, did not answer:

'Don't you know? Mara is so tall now that she's bigger than her own mother, and when I saw her again I couldn't believe that she was really the same person I used to go picking prickly pears with, and beating down walnuts.'

And he started singing in a loud voice all the songs he knew.

'Oh, Alfio, are you asleep?' he shouted when he had finished. 'Make sure that Whitey keeps behind you all the time. Be careful!'

'No, I'm not asleep!' replied Alfio hoarsely.

'Do you see the Pleiads which keep winking over there, towards Granvilla, as if they were sending off rockets for St Dominic too? It'll soon be daylight. We'll get to the fair in time to find a good spot. You there, my little black horse, you'll have a new halter, with red pompons, when we get to the fair! You too, Star!'

So he kept on talking to each of the horses in turn, so that they would be encouraged when they heard his voice in the dark. But he was sorry that Star and Little Blackie were going to the fair to be sold.

'When they're sold they'll go away with their new owner, and we won't see them any more in the herd, just like Mara when she went to Marineo.'

'Her father's doing nicely down there in Marineo. Because when I went to see them, they gave me bread, wine, cheese, and all God's plenty, because he's like the steward there now, and he has the keys to everything, and I could have eaten them out of house and home if I'd wanted to. Mara hardly knew me, it was so long since we'd seen each other! And she shouted out, "Oh, look! It's Jeli, who looks after the horses, you know, from Tebidi!" It's like when you come back from a long way away, and you've only got to see the top of a certain mountain to tell immediately that it's the place where you grew up.

Lia didn't want me to be too friendly to Mara, now that her daughter is grown up, because people who don't know any better would start talking. But Mara laughed, and looked as if she had just that instant been putting bread into the oven, she was so red. She laid the table, spreading the cloth on it, and didn't seem like the same person. "Don't you remember Tebidi any more then?" I asked her as soon as Lia had gone out to draw some fresh wine from the barrel. "Yes, yes, I do remember," she told me. "At Tebidi there was the bell and the bell tower that looked like the handle of a salt cellar, and the bell was rung from the gallery, and there were two stone cats too, purring on the gateway into the garden." I felt all those things inside me as she was talking about them. Mara looked me up and down with desire, and she kept saying, "How tall you are!" And then she started to laugh, and gave me a smack here on the head.'

That was how Jeli, the keeper of the horses, lost his livelihood, because just at that moment a carriage came up suddenly, which they had not heard before while it was climbing slowly up the slope, and it came on at a trot once it got to the level ground, with a great noise of whipping and bells, as if the devil were after it. The colts were terrified, and they scattered in a flash, so that it was like an earthquake, and there was a lot of calling, and shouting, and cries of Hey! Hey! Hey! from Jeli and the boy before they could gather them again round Whitey, who was herself trotting listlessly, with her bell round her neck. As soon as Jeli had counted the animals, he realised that Star was missing, and he ran his fingers through his hair, because at that spot the road ran alongside a ravine, and it was in that ravine that Star broke his back, a colt that was worth twelve onze, like twelve angels in heaven! He kept on weeping and calling out to the colt,

Hoy! Hoy!, but it was no longer to be seen. At long last Star answered from the bottom of the ravine, with a mournful neigh, as if it could speak, poor thing!

'Oh my God!' Jeli and the boy were crying out. 'This has ruined us! Oh my God!'

The travellers who were going to the fair, when they heard that weeping in the dark, asked what they had lost. And then, once they knew, they went on their way.

Star lay where he had fallen, with his hooves in the air, and while Jeli was feeling him all over, and talking to him as if he could make him understand, the poor beast lifted its neck with difficulty, and turned its head towards him, and it could be heard panting and quivering with pain.

'Something's probably broken!' whimpered Jeli, in despair because he could not see anything in the dark. And the colt, motionless as a stone, let its head fall again like a lump of lead. Alfio, who had stayed on the road to look after the herd, calmed down first and took his bread out of his bag. By now the sky had turned whitish, and all the mountains round were becoming visible one by one, black and high. At the bend of the road the village could be distinguished, with Calvary Hill and Windmill Hill standing out against the whiteness, but still hazy, and strewn with the white spots of the sheep. And, as the oxen which were feeding on the top of the hill against the blue of the sky moved to and fro, it seemed as if the outline of the mountain itself was quickening and swarming with life. From the bottom of the ravine the bell could no longer be heard, travellers had become scarcer and scarcer, and those few who did pass by were in a hurry to get to the fair. In that solitude, Jeli did not know which saint he should pray to. Alfio was no help at all by himself, and so he was just quietly nibbling his piece of bread.

At long last they saw the steward riding towards them, and shouting and cursing in the distance as he rushed along, when he saw the animals standing still on the road. And Alfio took to his heels over the hill. But Jeli did not move away from Star. The steward left his mule on the road, and he too went down into the ravine, trying to help the colt to get up and pulling it by the tail. 'Leave him alone!' said Jeli, his face as white as if he had broken his own back. 'Leave him alone! Can't you see he can't move, poor beast?'

And indeed, at every movement and every effort they forced him to make, Star emitted a rattle which made him sound human. The steward gave vent to his feelings by kicking and clouting Jeli, and swearing like a trooper. Then Alfio, feeling somewhat reassured, came back onto the road so as not to leave the horses unguarded, and he made an effort to excuse himself, saying, 'It's not my fault. I was going on ahead with Whitey.'

'There's nothing to be done here,' said the steward at last, certain by now that he was only wasting his time. 'All we can get from this is the skin, while it's still sound.'

Jeli started to tremble like a leaf when he saw the steward go to get his gun out of the mule's packsaddle. 'Clear off, you layabout!' the steward yelled at him. 'I don't know what's stopping me from laying you out by the side of that colt that's worth a lot more than you, with all the blasted baptising some lousy priest gave you!'

Star, not being able to move, turned his head with his great eyes wide open as if he had understood it all, and his hair bristled in waves all along his ribs, so that it seemed that he was shivering underneath. And so the steward killed Star on the spot, to get his skin at least, and the slight noise made in the living flesh by the point-blank shot was felt by Jeli inside himself.

'Now, if you want my advice,' were the steward's parting words, 'you won't show your face in front of the boss any more, and you won't ask for your wages, or else he'll give you more than wages to think about!'

The steward and Alfio went away, with the other colts which did not even turn to see where Star was left, and as they went they tugged at the grass along the side of the road. Star was left alone in the ravine, waiting for someone to come and skin him, with his eyes still wide open, and all four legs stretched out, for it was only now he was able to stretch them. Jeli, having seen how the steward had been capable of taking aim at the colt as it turned its head in such pain and such terror, and had had the heart to shoot, wept no more, and sat on a stone looking very hard at Star, until the men arrived to take the skin.

Now he could go off and amuse himself, and enjoy the feast-day, or stand in the square the whole day long, looking at the gentlemen in the café, which was what he liked best to do, since he had no livelihood any more, nowhere to live, and he had to look round for someone to employ him – if anyone would after that disaster with Star.

That's how things go in this world. While Jeli went round looking for employment, with his bag over his shoulder and his stick in his hand, the band were playing happily in the square, with feathers in their hats, in the middle of a crowd of white caps, as thick as flies, and gentlemen were enjoying it all sitting in the café. Everyone was dressed up for the feast, just like the animals at the fair, and in one corner of the square there was a woman in a short skirt and flesh-coloured stockings, which made it look as though her legs were bare, and she was beating on the big cash-box in front of a large painted sheet, on which there was a great slaughter of

Christians, with blood pouring out in torrents. And in the crowd looking at it open-mouthed there was also Farmer Cola, who had known Jeli since the time he was at Passanitello, and who said to Jeli that he would find him a job since Isidoro Macca was looking for someone to look after the pigs. 'But don't say anything about Star,' Farmer Cola warned him. 'Anyone at all can have a stroke of bad luck like that. But it's best to say nothing.'

So they went to look for Macca, who was at the dance, and while Farmer Cola was acting as ambassador, Jeli waited in the road, in the crowd that were looking through the shop door. In the bare room there were hundreds of people jumping about and enjoying themselves, all red and gasping for breath, and there was a great stamping of boots on the brick floor, so that you could not even hear the loud boom of the double bass. And as soon as one piece of music finished, which cost very little, they raised their hands as a sign that they wanted another, and the double-bass player made a cross in charcoal on the wall, to keep the account up to date, and they started off all over again. 'Those people in there are spending without thinking twice about it,' said Jeli, 'and that means they've got their pockets full, and they aren't in straits like me, without an employer. They're sweating and tiring themselves out and jumping about for pleasure, as though they were paid to do it!' Farmer Cola returned, saying that Macca did not need anyone. Then Jeli shrugged his shoulders and went away with a very heavy heart.

Mara lived in the direction of Sant'Antonio, where the houses clamber up the hill, facing the valley of the Canziria, all green with prickly pears, and with the mill wheels foaming on the valley floor in the torrent. But Jeli did not have the courage to go into those parts now that he was not wanted even to look after pigs, and as he mooched around in the middle of the crowd that was pushing and shoving him without a thought, he felt more alone than when he was with his colts on the moors of Passanitello, and he felt like weeping. At last in the square he came across Farmer Agrippino, who was wandering about with his arms swinging to and fro, enjoying the feast-day, and who shouted after him, 'Oh! Jeli! Hey!' and took him home with him. Mara was all dressed up, and her earrings were so long that they brushed her cheeks, and she was standing in the doorway, with her hands across her stomach, laden with rings, waiting for the dark so that she could go and see the fireworks.

'Oh!' Mara said to him. 'So you've come as well for the feast of St John!'

Jeli did not want to go in because he was so poorly dressed, but Farmer Agrippino pushed him in the shoulders saying that they were not seeing him for the first time, and that people knew that he had come for the fair with his boss's colts. Lia poured him a good glass of wine, and they insisted that he should go with them to see the illuminations, with their friends and neighbours.

When they got to the square Jeli gaped in wonder. The whole square looked like a sea of fire, just as when the stubble is set on fire, because of the great number of rockets which the faithful were letting off under the eyes of the saint, who was enjoying them from the entrance of the Rosary shrine, quite black beneath his silver canopy. The faithful were coming and going among the flames like so many devils, and there was even a poorly dressed woman, with unruly hair and eyes that seemed to stand out from her head, who was letting off rockets too, and a priest in a black cassock and without a hat, who seemed to be obsessed with devotion.

'That man there is the son of Farmer Neri, the steward in Salonia, and he's spent more than ten lire on fireworks!' said Lia, pointing to a young man who was going round the square holding two rockets at once in his hands, like two candles, so that all the women devoured him with their eyes, and cried out to him, 'Long live St John!'

'His father is rich and he's got more than twenty head of cattle,' added Farmer Agrippino.

Mara knew also that he had carried the big banner in the procession, and held it as straight as a ramrod, he was such a fine strong young man.

Farmer Neri's son seemed to have heard them, and lit his rockets for Mara, circling round her. And when the fireworks were over he accompanied them, and took them to the dance, and to the diorama which was showing the old world and the new world, and paid for them all, even for Jeli who walked behind the party like a dog without a master. He saw Farmer Neri's son dancing with Mara, who twisted round and bowed down like a dove on a roof, and held out the corner of her apron very nicely, while Farmer Neri's son leapt about like a colt, until Lia wept like a child in sheer delight, and Farmer Agrippino nodded his head in satisfaction, since things were going so well.

At last, when they were tired, they went wandering about in the main street, carried along by the crowd as though they were in a river in spate, and went to see the illuminated transparencies, which showed St John's head being cut off, which was enough to make a Turk weep, with the saint's legs kicking about like a young deer under the cleaver. Close by was the band, playing under a great illuminated wooden umbrella, and in the square there was such a great crowd that never had so many people been seen at the fair before.

Mara walked on the arm of Farmer Neri's son, like a young lady, and she spoke into his ear, and laughed as though she were really amused. Jeli was so tired he could not walk any more, and he sat down on the pavement and slept there until he was awakened by the fireworks' first maroons. Mara was at that moment by the side of Farmer Neri's son, leaning against him with her hands clasped on his shoulder, and in the coloured light of the fireworks she was one instant pure white and the next instant bright red. When the last flights of rockets were flying through the sky, Farmer Neri's son turned to her, with his green face, and gave her a kiss.

Jeli said nothing, but at that moment the whole feast, which he had enjoyed up to then, turned into poison for him, and he began to think again of all his misfortunes, which had gone out of his mind. He was left without a master, and he no longer knew what to do, or where to go, and he had no bread and no home any more, and the dogs could eat him like Star left at the bottom of the ravine, skinned right down to his hooves.

Meanwhile all round him people were still making a hullabaloo even though it was now dark, and Mara and her friends were skipping and singing along the stony little lane as they returned home.

'Goodnight! Goodnight!' her friends kept on saying, one by one, as they parted.

Mara said good night as if she were singing, there was so much happiness in her voice, and Farmer Neri's son really seemed as if he would never let her go, while Farmer Agrippino and Lia were quarrelling as they opened the door of their home. No one bothered about Jeli, until Farmer Agrippino remembered him and asked him:

'Where are you going now?'

'I don't know,' said Jeli.

'Come to see me tomorrow, and I'll help you get a job. For tonight go back to the square where we've just been listening to the band. You'll find a place on some bench, and you must be used to sleeping in the open.'

Jeli certainly was used to that, but what troubled him was that Mara had said nothing to him and had left him standing on the doorstep like a tramp. And the next day, when he came to see Farmer Agrippino, as soon as he was alone with the girl he said:

'Oh Mara! How you forget your friends!'

'Oh, is that you Jeli?' said Mara. 'No, I didn't forget you, but I was so tired after the fireworks!'

'But you do like him, Farmer Neri's son?' he asked, twisting and turning the stick in his hands.

'What kind of talk is this?' replied Mara brusquely. 'My mother's not far away and she'll hear everything.'

Farmer Agrippino found him a job as a shepherd at Salonia, where Farmer Neri was the steward, but since Jeli had little experience in that work he had to be happy with a big drop in pay.

Now he took care of his sheep, and learned how to make cheese and ricotta and *caciocavallo*[6], and other dairy products. But in the talk every evening in the farmyard with the other shepherds and peasants, while the women were shelling beans for soup, if the conversation turned on Farmer Neri's son, who was going to marry Farmer Agrippino's Mara, Jeli stopped talking, and he did not dare to open his mouth again. Once when the field-warden was teasing him, saying that Mara did not want anything more to do with him, after everyone had been saying that they would become husband and wife, Jeli, who was watching the pot in which he was boiling the milk, said as he gently dissolved the rennet:

'Mara is more beautiful now that she's grown up, and she's like a young lady.'

However, since he was patient and hard-working, he quickly learnt everything to do with his job better than one born into it, and since he was used to being with animals he loved his sheep as if they were his own. And so the 'sickness' did not play too much havoc at Salonia, and the flock prospered, so that Farmer Neri was delighted every time he came to the farm, and in the new year he was persuaded to induce the master to raise Jeli's pay, so that he came to have almost as much as he had had when he looked after the horses. And that was money well spent, for Jeli did not stop to count the miles and miles he went looking for the best pasture for his animals. And if the sheep were in labour or were sick, he took them out to pasture inside the saddle-bags on the donkey, and he carried the lambs on his shoulders, bleating into his face with their muzzles poking out of the bag, and they sucked his ears as though they were suckling. In the famous snowfall of the night of St Lucia the snow fell four feet deep in the Dead Lake at Salonia, and when the day broke there was nothing else to be seen for miles and miles all round. And not even the sheep's ears would have been visible, if Jeli had not got up three or four times in the night to chase them round the field until the poor beasts shook the snow off their backs and so did not end up buried like so many of the neighbouring flocks. That is what Farmer Agrippino said when he came to cast an eye on the small field of broad beans which he had at Salonia. And he said also that that tale about Farmer Neri's son going to marry his daughter Mara had no truth in it, for Mara had other ideas in her head.

'People said they were going to get married at Christmas,' said Jeli.

'There's no truth in it. No one's getting married. It's all the idle gossip of envious people who poke their noses into other people's affairs,' answered Farmer Agrippino.

However, the field-warden, who knew a thing or two, having heard it spoken about on the square, when he went to the village on Sundays, said how things really were, once Farmer Agrippino had gone away. They were not getting married any more because Farmer Neri's son had got to know that Farmer Agrippino's Mara had been carrying on with Don Alfonso, the young squire, who had known Mara as a child. And Farmer Neri had said that his son wanted to be as respected as his father was, and that he did not want any horns in his house except those of his oxen.

Jeli was there too, sitting in a circle with the others at breakfast, and at that moment he was slicing the bread. He said nothing, but he lost his appetite for that day.

While he was taking his sheep to pasture he thought once more of Mara when she was a little girl, how they were together all day long and went into the Jacitano Valley and onto the Hill of the Cross, and she stood watching him with her chin tilted up while he clambered up to the treetops for birds' nests. And he thought also about Don Alfonso who used to come to visit him from the nearby villa, and how they would stretch out prone on the grass to tickle the crickets' nests with straws. He went on turning these things over and over in his mind for hours and hours, sitting on the edge of the ditch with his knees between his arms – the tall walnut trees at Tebidi, and the thick bushes in the valley, and the sides of the hills green with sumac, and the grey olive trees leaning against each other in the valley like mist, and the red roof of the big building, and the bell tower 'that looked like the handle of a salt cellar' among the oranges in the garden. Here, on the other hand, the countryside stretched out in front of him bare and deserted, with patches of parched grass, shading away silently into the distant suffocating air.

In the spring, as soon as the bean pods began to bend their heads, Mara came to Salonia with her father and mother, and the boy and the donkey, to harvest the beans, and they came all together to sleep at the farmhouse for those two or three days that the harvesting lasted. And so Jeli saw the girl morning and evening, and they often sat side by side on the wall of the sheepfold, chatting together while the boy counted the sheep. 'It's like being back at Tebidi,' said Mara, 'when we were little, and we were on the little bridge by the lane.'

Jeli remembered all that too, even though he said nothing because he was a prudent boy of few words.

When the harvest was over, the evening before they left, Mara came to say goodbye to the youth, while he was making the ricotta and was intent on gathering the whey in the ladle. 'I'm saying goodbye to you now,' she told him, 'because tomorrow we're going back to Vizzini.'

'How have the beans gone?'

'Badly! They've all been eaten up by dry rot this year.'

'They need rain and there hasn't been much,' said Jeli. 'We've been forced to kill all the lambs because there was nothing for them to eat. Right across Salonia there's not been three inches of grass.'

'But that doesn't matter much to you. You always get your wages, in good years and in bad!'

'Yes, that's true,' he said, 'but I'm sorry to have to deliver these poor beasts into the hands of the butcher.'

'You remember when you came for the feast of St John, and you were left without any work?'

'Yes, I remember.'

'It was my father who got you a job here, with Farmer Neri.'

'And you, why didn't you marry Farmer Neri's son?'

'Because it wasn't God's will. My father's been unlucky,' she went on after a short pause. 'Since we've been at Marineo everything's turned out badly. The beans, the wheat, that little bit of a vineyard we've got up there. Then my brother has gone for a soldier, and a mule died too that was worth forty onze.'

'I know,' answered Jeli. 'The bay mule.'

'Now that we've lost all we had, who'd want to marry me?'

Mara was breaking a twig of blackthorn into little pieces, while she spoke, with her chin leaning on her breast, and her eyes lowered, and she rubbed her elbow against Jeli's elbow, without realising she was doing it. But Jeli, with his eyes fixed on the churn, said nothing either, and she went on:

'At Tebidi they used to say that we would be husband and wife. Do you remember?'

'Yes,' said Jeli, and he placed the ladle on the side of the churn. 'But I'm a poor shepherd, and I can't hope to get a farmer's daughter like you.'

Mara was silent for a moment, and then she said:

'If you want me, I'd be glad to take you.'

'Really?'

'Yes, really.'

'And what would Farmer Agrippino say?'

'My father says that you know your job now, and you're not one of those who go and spend all their pay, but you turn one penny into two, and you don't eat much, and so you will come to have sheep of your own, and get rich.'

'If that's the way it is,' concluded Jeli, 'then I'll be glad to take you too.'

'Now!' Mara said to him, when it was dark and the sheep were falling silent one by one. 'If you want a kiss now, I'll give you one, because we're going to be husband and wife.'

41

Jeli received her kiss in blissful silence, and then, not knowing what else to say, said:

'I have always loved you, even when you wanted to leave me for Farmer Neri's son. But I didn't have the heart to ask you about the other fellow.'

'Don't you see? We were meant for each other!' concluded Mara.

Farmer Agrippino did in fact say yes, and Lia very quickly got together a new jacket and a pair of velvet breeches for their son-in-law. Mara was as beautiful and fresh as a rose, with that white cape which made her look like an Easter lamb, and with that amber necklace against which her neck seemed so white. And so when Jeli walked along the road at her side, he was as stiff as a poker, all dressed up in new cloth and velvet, and he did not dare to blow his nose with his handkerchief of red silk, lest he should be stared at, and the neighbours and all those who knew about Don Alfonso laughed in his face. When Mara said 'I do,' and the priest gave her to him as his wife with a great sign of the cross, Jeli took her home, and it seemed to him that they had given him all the gold of the Madonna and all the land his eyes had ever seen.

'Now that we are husband and wife,' he said to her when they were at home, and he sat facing her very humbly, 'now that we are husband and wife I can tell you that I didn't think you would want to have me… while you could have had so many better than me… so beautiful and graceful as you are!…'

The poor chap did not know what else to say to her, and he was beside himself with happiness seeing Mara around the house, touching everything and tidying everything up, and being the mistress of the house. He could hardly drag himself away from the house to return to Salonia. When Monday came, he took a long time arranging his saddle-bags and his cloak and his waxed umbrella on the donkey's packsaddle. 'You ought to come to Salonia too!' he said to his wife who was watching him from the threshold. 'You ought to come with me.' But the woman started to laugh, and answered that she was not born to keep sheep, and had nothing to go to Salonia for.

Mara was certainly not born to keep sheep, and she was not used to the north wind of January, when hands go stiff with cold as they rest on a stick, and nails feel as though they are falling out, or to the furious rainstorms when the water penetrates right into the bones, or to the suffocating dust on the roads, when the sheep are travelling under the blazing sun, or to the hard pallet and the mouldy bread, or to the long, silent, solitary days, when in the parched countryside there is nothing to be seen in the distance except, very rarely, some sun-blackened peasant driving his silent donkey in front of him along the white, interminable road.

At least Jeli knew that Mara was warm beneath the blankets, or spinning by the fire, or chatting with a group of neighbours, or enjoying the sun on the balcony, while he was returning from pasture tired and thirsty, or drenched with rain, or when the wind was blowing the snow into the hut and extinguishing the fire of vine shoots. Every month Mara went to draw his salary from the master, and she did not lack for eggs in the hen house, or oil in the lamp, or wine in the bottle. And twice a month Jeli came to see her, and she waited for him on the balcony, distaff in hand. And when he had tied the donkey in the stable, and taken its packsaddle off, and put some fodder for it in the manger, and put the wood in the shelter in the yard, or put the things he was bringing into the kitchen, Mara helped him to hang his cloak on the nail, and to take off his leather leggings by the fire, and poured his wine for him, and put the soup on to boil, and set the table, very quietly and providently like a good housewife, all the time telling him about this and that, about the hen which she had put to brood, about the cloth on the loom, about the calf she was bringing up, without forgetting any of the things she had to do. When he was at home Jeli felt he was better off than the Pope.

But on St Barbara's night he came home at an unusual hour, when all the lights were off in the lane, and the town clock was striking midnight. He was coming because the mare that the owner had left in the meadow had suddenly fallen sick, and it was obvious that this was something that needed the farrier immediately, and it took some doing to get the mare to the village, with the rain falling in torrents, and the roads where you sank up to your knees. Even though he knocked loudly and called out to Mara to come to the door, he had to wait half an hour under the eaves till he was drenched. At long last his wife came to open up for him, and then she began to abuse him worse than if she had been the one who had had to rush through the fields in that dreadful weather. 'What's the matter with you?' he asked her.

'What's wrong is that you've frightened me, coming home at this hour! What time do you call this for a human creature? I'll be ill tomorrow!'

'Go and lie down. I'll light the fire.'

'No, I need to get some wood.'

'I'll go.'

'No, I'm telling you.'

When Mara came back with the wood in her arms, Jeli asked her:

'Why did you open the door of the yard? Wasn't there any more wood in the kitchen?'

44

'No, I went to get it from the shelter.'

She let herself be kissed, but very coldly, and she turned her head away.

'His wife lets him get soaked through outside,' said the neighbours, 'while she has a cuckoo in the nest with her!'

But Jeli knew nothing about being a cuckold, and nobody bothered to tell him, because it was not something that mattered to him, and he had taken the fallen woman, after Farmer Neri's son had abandoned her when he knew about Don Alfonso. Jeli, on the other hand, was living happily and contented, despite the disgrace, and he was getting as fat as a pig, 'because horns are thin, but they keep the home fat!'

Finally one day the boy who worked with the flock said it to his face when they came to blows over the pieces of cheese which were found to have had bits taken out of them. 'Now that Don Alfonso has taken your wife, you think you're his brother-in-law, and you put on airs as if you were a crowned king with those horns on your head.'

The steward and the field-warden expected to see blood flow after these words. But Jeli was left stupefied, as if he had not heard, or as if it was nothing to do with him, and he pulled such an ox-like face that horns would have suited him very well.

Now it was getting near Easter-time, and the steward sent all the workers on the farm to confession, hoping that out of fear of God they would not steal any more. Jeli went too, and when he came out of church he sought out the boy who had said those words, and threw his arm round his shoulder, saying to him:

'The confessor told me to pardon you, but I'm not angry with you for talking as you did. And if you don't take pieces out of the cheese any more, it doesn't matter to me what you said when you were annoyed.'

From that moment on they gave him the nickname of Golden Horns, and he kept that nickname, he and all his family, even after he had washed those horns in blood.

Mara had been to confession too, and she came back from church all wrapped up in her cape, and with her eyes on the ground, looking like a Mary Magdalene. Jeli, who was silently waiting for her on the balcony, when he saw her coming like that, looking as if she had the Body of the Lord inside her, went pale and stood looking at her from head to foot, as if he were seeing her for the first time, or as if they had changed his Mara. And he hardly dared to raise his eyes to her, while she was spreading the cloth and putting the bowls on the table, as peaceful and clean as usual.

Then, after he had thought about it for a long while, he asked her:

'Is it true that you're carrying on with Don Alfonso?'

Mara stared at him with her very dark large eyes, and made the sign of the cross. 'Why do you want to make me sin on this very day?' she exclaimed.

'I didn't believe it, because we were always together with Don Alfonso when we were children, and not a day passed without his coming to Tebidi, when he was staying in the country nearby. And then he's rich, he's got pots of money, and if he wanted women he could get married, and he wouldn't be short of anything to eat, or anything at all.'

But Mara was getting angry, and she started to abuse him so roughly that the poor fellow did not dare to raise his face from his plate.

Finally, so that the food which God had sent and which they were eating should not turn into poison, Mara changed the subject, and asked him if he had thought about hoeing that little bit of flax which they had sown in the bean field.

'Yes,' Jeli replied, 'the flax will do well.'

'If that's so,' said Mara, 'then this winter I'll make you two new shirts to keep you warm.'

In short, Jeli did not know what the word cuckold meant, and he did not know what jealousy was. It was hard for him to get any new idea into his head, and this was such a big one that it was the devil's own job to get his head round it, particularly when he had Mara in front of his eyes, so beautiful, so white, so clean. And then she herself had wanted him. And she had been in his mind for years and years, since he was a boy. And when they had told him she was going to marry someone else, he had not had the heart to eat or drink for the whole of that day. And even when he thought about Don Alfonso, whom he had been together with so many times, and who had always brought him sweets and white bread, he still seemed to see him all the time in his new clothes, with his curly hair, and his face as white and smooth as a girl's. And since he had not seen him afterwards, because he was a poor shepherd and spent the whole year in the fields, he had always had that picture of him in his heart. But the first time that, unluckily for him, he saw him again after so many years, Jeli felt his stomach turn over. Don Alfonso was now tall, so that he no longer looked like the same person, and now he had a fine beard which was curly like his hair, and a velvet jacket, and a gold chain across his paunch. However, he recognised Jeli, and slapped him on the back as he said hello. He had come with the owner of the farm, together with a crowd of friends, for a trip into the country at shearing-time. And Mara had suddenly decided to come too, on the pretext that she was pregnant and had a yearning for fresh ricotta.

It was a beautifully hot day, in the white fields, with the hedges in bloom, and the long files of vines, and the sheep

47

were leaping about and bleating with pleasure at being relieved of all that wool, and in the kitchen the women were building up a large fire to cook all the food the master had brought for dinner. Meanwhile the gentlemen who were waiting for their dinner had gone into the shade, under the carobs, and had tambourines and bagpipes playing, and were dancing with the women of the farm, and they seemed to be getting on well together. Jeli, as he went on shearing the sheep, felt something inside him, he did not know why – like a thorn, like a nail, like a very small pair of scissors working away internally – like a poison. The master had ordered them to slaughter two kids, a year-old wether, some chickens, and a turkey. It was clear he wanted to do things in a big way, without counting the cost, to distinguish himself among his friends. And while all these beasts were squealing with pain, and the kids were screaming under the knife, Jeli felt his knees trembling, and at times it seemed to him as if the wool he was shearing and the grass in which the sheep were leaping about were flaming with blood.

'Don't go!' he told Mara, as Don Alfonso was calling to her to come and dance with the others. 'Don't go, Mara!'

'Why not?'

'Because I don't want you to go. Don't go!'

'You can hear them calling me.'

He did not come out with any more audible words, but remained bent over the sheep he was shearing. Mara shrugged her shoulders, and went off to dance. She was flushed and happy, and her black eyes shone like stars, and she laughed and revealed her white teeth, and all the gold she was wearing tossed and glittered on her cheeks and breast, and she looked like the Virgin Mary herself. Jeli had straightened his back, with his long shears in his hand, and his face was as white as his father's, the cowherd, when he was shivering with fever by the fire in the hut. All at once, when he saw Don Alfonso, with his fine curly beard and his velvet jacket and his gold chain on his paunch, take Mara by the hand to dance with her – only then, when he saw him touch her, did he fling himself at him and cut his throat with one stroke, as he would a young goat.

Later, when they were taking him before the judge, bound and overcome without having offered the least resistance, he said:

'What! Didn't I have to kill him? If he'd taken Mara from me!...'

Nasty Foxfur

He was called Nasty Foxfur because he had red hair. And he had red hair because he was a bad, malicious boy, who gave every promise of ending up a complete villain. And so all the men at the red-sand pit called him Foxfur. And even his mother, hearing him called that so often, had almost forgotten the name he was baptised by.

Besides, she only saw him on Saturday evenings, when he came home with those few coins he had earned during the week. And because he was a redhead it was also to be feared that he had kept a few of those coins back for himself. So, to clear up any doubt, his elder sister welcomed him home with a box on the ear.

However, the boss of the pit had confirmed that he was paid so much and no more. And in all conscience even that was too much for Foxfur, a dirty little brat whom nobody wanted around, and whom everyone shunned like a mangy dog, and stroked with his foot when he came within range.

He really was an ugly customer, surly, ill-tempered, and wild. At midday, when all the other workers in the pit were sitting together having their soup and a bit of a break, he used to go off and hide in a corner, with his basket between his knees, to gnaw away at his ration of bread, as all animals do. And all the others had a go at jeering at him, and threw stones at him, until the foreman sent him back to work with a kick. He thrived between kicks, and let himself be more heavily burdened than the grey donkey, without daring to complain. He was always ragged and filthy with red sand, since his sister had got engaged, and had other things to bother about. Nevertheless, he was so well known throughout Monserrato and Carvana that the pit where he worked was known as 'Foxfur's pit', which was a source of considerable annoyance to the owner. The fact is that they kept him on as an act of charity and because the skilled workman Misciu, his father, had died in the pit.

This is how he died. One Saturday he had wanted to finish a certain job which he had taken on as piece-work. This was to demolish a pillar which had been left standing some time back as a support for the roof of the pit, and which was no longer needed now, and which he and the boss had roughly calculated to contain thirty-five or forty loads of sand. In fact, Misciu dug for three days, and there was still enough left to last for half of Monday. It had been a poor deal, and only a simpleton like Misciu would let himself be imposed upon in this way by the boss. That is precisely why they called him Misciu the Jackass, and he was the beast of burden for the whole pit. He, poor devil that he was, let them go on talking and was content to scrape a living with his two hands, rather than turn them on his workmates and pick a quarrel. Foxfur used to pull a face, as if all those impositions fell upon his shoulders, and, little as he was, he gave such looks as made the others say: 'Get away! You won't die in your bed, like your father.'

However, his father did not die in his bed either, even though he was a good-natured jackass. Uncle Mommu, who was crippled, had said that that pillar there, he wouldn't have taken it away, not for twenty onze, it was so dangerous. But, on the other hand, everything is dangerous in the pit, and if you are going to bother about danger, then you had better go and be a lawyer.

So on that Saturday evening Misciu was still scraping away at his pillar quite a while after the angelus had rung and all his workmates had lit their pipes and gone off, telling him to have fun slaving his guts out for love of the boss, and advising him not to die like a rat in a trap. He was used to mockery and paid no attention to them, responding merely with the ugh! ugh! of the full-blooded blows of his mattock. As he worked he muttered, 'That's for bread! That's for wine! That's for a skirt for Nunziata!' And so he went on, keeping count of how he would spend the money for what he called his 'contract', this piece-worker!

Outside the pit the sky was swarming with stars, and down there the lantern was smoking and spinning like a top. And the huge red pillar, ripped open by the blows of the mattock, twisted itself and bent over as though it had stomach ache and were saying, 'Ugh! Ah!' Foxfur kept clearing the ground round it, and put the pickaxe, the empty sack, and the flask of wine in a safe place. His father, who loved him, the poor little fellow, kept on saying to him, 'Keep away!' or 'Watch out! Watch out, in case any bits of stone or lumps of sand fall down!' All of a sudden he stopped speaking, and Foxfur, who had turned to replace the tools in the basket, heard a dull, suffocated noise, such as the sand makes when it comes down all at once, and the light went out.

That evening, when they rushed to find the engineer who directed the work at the pit, they found him at the theatre. He would not have exchanged his seat in the stalls there for a throne, for he was a great enthusiast. Rossi was putting on *Hamlet*, and there was a very good audience. All the poor women of Monserrato were in a circle round the door, shrieking and beating their breasts to announce the great misfortune which had befallen Santa. She, poor woman, was the only one who was not saying anything, but her teeth were chattering as if it were January. The engineer, when they told him that the accident had happened about four hours ago, asked them what was the use of coming to him after four hours. All the same, he went there with ladders and wind-proof torches, but that took another two hours, which made six altogether, and the lame man said that it would take a week to clear the underground passage of all the stuff that had fallen into it.

There certainly were more than forty cartloads of sand! A whole mountain of sand had fallen, all very fine and burnt by the lava, so that it could have been worked into mortar with the hands alone, and it would take two parts of lime to one of sand. There was enough there to fill carts for weeks. A fine bit of business for Jackass!

The engineer went back to see Ophelia buried, and the other miners shrugged their shoulders and went back home one by one. With such a crowd and all the chatter no one took any notice of a boy's voice, which had nothing human in it, and which screamed, 'Dig! Dig here! Now!' 'Look!' said the lame man. 'It's Foxfur! Where did Foxfur spring from? If you hadn't been Foxfur, you wouldn't have escaped. No, you wouldn't!' The others started to laugh, and someone said that Foxfur had the devil's own luck, and someone else said that he had nine lives like a cat. Foxfur did not reply, he did not even weep, he dug with his fingernails in the sand there, inside the hole, so that no one noticed him. And when they came near him with the light they saw such a distorted face, such glassy eyes, and such foam around his mouth as to inspire fear. His fingernails were torn out and hung from his hands all covered in blood. When they tried to pull him away, it became a nasty business. Since he could no longer scratch, he bit them like a mad dog, and they had to seize him by the hair to drag him away by main force.

However, he did come back to the pit after a few days. His whimpering mother led him there by the hand, since the bread you eat does not grow on trees. Indeed, he did not want to keep away from that gallery in the pit, and he dug there relentlessly, as if he were lifting every basket of sand off his father's chest. At times, while he was digging, he stopped suddenly with his mattock in the air, his face grim and his eyes rolling, and it looked as though he had stopped to listen to something which his demon was whispering in his ears, from the other side of the mountain of fallen sand. In those days he was so much more sad and wicked than usual that he hardly ate, and threw his bread to the dog, as if it were not one of God's gifts. The dog liked him, because dogs do not bite the hand that feeds them. But the grey donkey! It was on that poor, emaciated, and bandy-legged beast that Foxfur vented all his wickedness. He beat it without mercy, with the handle of his mattock, and muttered, 'You'll kick the bucket all the sooner!'

After his father's death it seemed as if the devil had got into him, and he worked like those ferocious buffaloes which have to be held by an iron ring through the nose. Knowing that he was Foxfur, he was prepared to be as bad as he could be, and if an accident occurred, or if a workman mislaid his tools, or a donkey broke a leg, or part of the gallery fell away, they always knew it was his doing. And in fact he took all the blows without complaining, just like the donkeys, which take them and arch their backs but go on doing things in their own way. With the other boys too he was downright cruel, and it seemed as if he wanted to avenge on those weaker than himself all the wrong which he imagined they had done to him and to his father. He certainly took a strange delight in recalling in detail all the ill-treatment and abuse to which they had subjected his father, and the way in which they had let him die. And when he was alone he would mutter, 'They're doing the same to me too! And they called my father Jackass because he didn't do the same to them!' And once, when the boss was passing by, he said, giving him a dirty look, 'He was the one who did it, for a few coppers!' And on another occasion, behind the lame man's back, 'And him too! And he started to laugh! I heard him, that evening!'

In a refinement of malignity he seemed to have taken under his wing a poor little lad, who had recently come to work in the pit, and who had dislocated his thigh in a fall from a bridge and was no longer able to be a bricklayer's labourer. The poor little fellow, when he was carrying his basket of sand on his shoulder, hobbled so much that he seemed to be dancing the tarantella, and that made all the men in the pit laugh. And that is why they gave him the name of Frog. However, working underground, frog though he was, he did manage to scrape a living, and Foxfur even gave him some of his bread, to have the pleasure of tyrannising over him, it was thought.

In fact he tormented him in a hundred different ways. At times he beat him without cause and without mercy, and if Frog did not defend himself, he beat him harder, and more furiously, and said to him, 'Take that, jackass! A jackass is what you are! If you haven't got the guts to defend yourself against someone who doesn't even hate you, it means that you'll let every Tom, Dick, and Harry walk all over you!'

Or when Frog was wiping away the blood which was coming out of his mouth and nose: 'So, if it hurts you to be beaten, you'll learn to hit back!' When Foxfur was driving a donkey up the steep slope which led from underground, and he saw it dig its heels in, exhausted, its back bending under the weight, panting and dull-eyed, he would beat it without mercy, with the handle of his mattock, and the blows sounded hard and dry on its shins and its bare ribs. Sometimes a beast would bend itself double under the beating, but then, exhausted, be unable to take another step, and fall on its knees. There was one which had fallen so many times that it had two wounds on its legs. Then Foxfur confided to Frog, 'A donkey gets beaten because it can't hit back. If it could hit back, it would trample us underfoot and tear our flesh off with its teeth.'

Or else he would say, 'When it comes to blows, make sure that you hit as hard as you can, and then those you hit will think you're better than they are, and you'll have so much less to put up with.'

When he was working with pick or mattock he moved his limbs furiously, as though he really had it in for the sand, and he struck and struck again with clenched teeth, and with that ugh! ugh! sound which his father had made. 'Sand is treacherous,' he whispered to Frog. 'It's just like all the others. If you're weaker, then it walks all over you, and if you're stronger, or if there are a lot of you (which is how the lame man works), then it gives up. My father was always striking it, and he never struck anyone but the sand, so they called him Jackass, and the sand swallowed him up treacherously, because it was stronger than he was.'

Every time that Frog had to do some work that was too heavy for him, and was whimpering like a chit of a girl, Foxfur struck him on the back and told him off, saying, 'Shut up, you sissy!' And if Frog did not stop whimpering, he gave him a hand, saying with some pride, 'Let me do it. I'm stronger than you.' Or else he gave him his half onion, and was happy to eat his own bread with nothing on it, and shrugged his shoulders, adding, 'I'm used to it.'

And he was used to everything – to boxes on the ear, to

kicks, to blows with the handle of a shovel, or with a pack-saddle strap, to seeing himself cursed and made fun of by everyone, to sleeping on stones, with his arms and his back worn out by fourteen hours' work. He was even used to being hungry, when the boss punished him by taking his bread and soup away from him. He used to say that his allowance of blows was the one thing his boss had never taken away from him, but of course blows didn't cost anything. He never complained however, and he got his revenge on the sly, by trickery, pulling one of those strokes which made it seem as though the devil was in him. And so he always brought down the punishment on himself even when he was not the guilty party. If he was not guilty, he was quite capable of it, and he never tried to excuse himself, since that would have been pointless anyway. And sometimes when Frog was terrified and pleaded with him in tears to tell the truth and prove himself innocent, he repeated, 'What's the good? I'm Foxfur!' And no one could tell whether that continual bowing of his head and shoulders came from sullen pride or desperate resignation, or whether he was by nature savage or timid. What is for sure is that his mother had never received a caress from him, and so she never gave him one.

As soon as he arrived home on Saturday evenings, with his ugly face spattered with freckles and red sand, and those rags of clothes hanging all over him, his sister grabbed the broom-handle if he presented himself at the door in that get-up, for it would have made her young man take to flight if he had seen what kind of brother-in-law he had to put up with. His mother was always at some neighbour's house or other, and so he went and curled up on his straw mattress like a sick dog. And so on Sundays, when all the other boys in the neighbourhood put on clean shirts to go to Mass, or to romp about outside, he seemed to have no other pastime but to go wandering through the orchards, hunting and stoning the poor lizards, which had done nothing to him, or damaging the hedges of prickly pears. Anyway, he did not like the jokes and stone-throwing of the other boys.

Misciu's widow was in despair at having such a bad character for a son, for such everyone said he was. And in fact he was reduced to the condition of those dogs which, by dint of getting kicked and having stones thrown at them by everyone, finish by putting their tails between their legs and running away from everyone they come across, and end up famished, with no fur on their bodies, and as wild as wolves. At least, underground in the sandpit, ugly and ragged and unkempt as he was, they did not make fun of him any more, and he seemed to have made on purpose for that job, even down to the colour of his hair, and those baleful nocturnal eyes that blinked if they saw the sun. There are donkeys like that, which work in the pits for years and years without ever getting out, and in those galleries where the pit shaft is vertical they let them down on ropes, and they stay there as long as they live. They are old donkeys, it is true, bought for only twelve or thirteen lire when they are about to be taken to the Plaja to be strangled. But they are still good for the work which they have to do down there in the pit. And Foxfur was certainly worth no more than they were, and if he did come out of the pit on Saturday evenings, that was because he had hands which enabled him to climb the rope, and he had to go and take his mother his week's pay.

He would certainly have preferred to be a bricklayer's labourer, as Frog had been, and sing while he worked on bridges, up in the air, in the middle of the bright blue sky, with the sun on his back, or to be a carter, like Gaspare who came to take the sand away from the pit, drowsily lounging on the shafts of his cart, with his pipe in his mouth, travelling all day long on the lovely country roads. Or better still he would have liked to be a peasant spending his life in the fields, in the middle of green things, under the leafy carob trees, with the sea in the background, deep blue in colour, and birdsong overhead. But mining had been his father's trade, and it was the trade he had been born into. And as he thought about all that, he showed Frog the pillar that had fallen on his father, and which still provided fine, burnt sand which the carter came to load onto his cart, with his pipe in his mouth and lounging on the shafts of his cart. And he said that when they had finished digging they would find his father's body, which should be wearing fustian breeches that were almost new. Frog was afraid, but he was not. He told how he had always been there, from when he was a child, and had always seen that black hole which plunged down into the earth, and into which his father used to take him by the hand. Then he spread his arms out to right and left, and described how the intricate labyrinth of the galleries spread out everywhere below their feet, in this direction and that, even to where they could see the black and desolate lava waste, grimy with scorched broom. And he told how so many men had ended up either squashed to death or lost in the darkness, and that they had been walking for years and were still walking without managing to find the ventilation shaft by which they had entered, and without being able to hear the despairing cries of their children searching for them in vain.

But once, when they were filling the baskets, they found one of Misciu's shoes, and Foxfur was seized with such a fit of trembling that they had to pull him up into the open air on ropes, just like a donkey that was about to breathe its last. However, they could not find either his almost-new breeches or what was left of Misciu himself, even though the experts insisted that that must be the exact spot where the pillar had fallen on top of him. And some workmen, new to the job, remarked upon the curious fact that the sand was capricious, knocking Jackass about here and there, and sending his shoes in one direction and his feet in another.

After that shoe was found, Foxfur was seized with such a fear of seeing his father's bare foot also appear in the sand that he refused to give another blow with his mattock. They hit him on the head with it. He went to work in another section of the gallery, and refused to go back to that place again. Two or three days afterwards they did in fact discover Misciu's corpse, still wearing the breeches, and stretched out face-down, looking as though he were embalmed. Uncle Mommu observed that he must have found it hard to die, because the pillar had bent in an arch over him and had buried him alive. It was even possible to see still how Misciu had tried instinctively to get free by burrowing in the sand, and his hands were lacerated and his fingernails broken. 'Just like his son Foxfur,' said the lame man. 'He was digging away in here, while his son was digging out there.' But they said nothing to the boy, because they knew that he was malignant and vengeful.

The carter cleared the corpse out of the workings in the same way as he cleared the fallen sand and the dead donkeys, only this time, in addition to the stink of the carcass, there was the fact that this was 'baptised flesh'. And the widow cut the breeches and the shirt down to fit Foxfur, who was thus for the first time dressed in almost-new clothes. And the shoes were put away for when he had grown more, since it is not possible to cut shoes down to size, and his sister's fiancé had not wanted the shoes of a dead man.

Whenever Foxfur stroked these almost-new fustian breeches

on his legs, he thought they were as soft and smooth as his father's hands when they used to stroke his hair, rough and red as it was. He kept these shoes hung on a nail in his straw mattress, as if they had been the Pope's slippers, and on Sundays he took them in his hands, and polished them, and tried them on for size. Then he put them on the ground side by side, and stayed contemplating them, with his elbows on his knees and his chin in his hands, for hours on end, turning over who knows what ideas in that nasty brain of his.

He did have some strange ideas did Foxfur! Since he had also inherited his father's pickaxe and mattock, he used them, even though they were too heavy for someone of his age. And when they asked him if he wanted to sell them, and said they would pay him for them as though they were new, he said no, his father had made their handles so smooth and shiny with his own hands, and he could not make any others more smooth and shiny, even if he had used them for hundreds and hundreds of years.

By then the grey donkey had died of hard work and old age, and the carter had carried it off to fling it onto the lava waste far away. 'That's what they do,' muttered Foxfur. 'Things that are no use to them any more they just fling away into the distance.' He paid a visit to the corpse of the grey donkey in the bottom of the gorge, and he forced Frog to go with him, even though Frog did not want to go. And Foxfur told him that in this world you had to get used to looking everything in the face, whether it was beautiful or ugly. And he watched with the keen curiosity of a dirty little brat the dogs which came running from all the farms around to fight over the grey donkey's flesh. The dogs ran off yelping when the boys appeared, and they roamed about and whined on the crags opposite, but the redhead did not allow Frog to drive them away by stoning them. 'You see that black bitch,' he said to him, 'that one that isn't afraid of your stones? She isn't afraid because she's more hungry than the others. You see those ribs on her?' Now the grey donkey was not suffering any more, but lay there quietly with its four legs stretched out, and allowed the dogs to enjoy themselves emptying out its eye sockets and stripping the flesh off its white bones. And the teeth that were tearing at its entrails could not make it arch its back as the slightest blow of a shovel used to when they gave him one to put some energy into his body when he was climbing up the steep track from the pit. That's how things go! The grey donkey too had had blows from mattocks and sores on its neck from its harness, and it too, when it was bent beneath its burden, without the breath to carry on, had that look in its eyes, even while they were beating it, that seemed to say, 'No more! No more!' But now those eyes were being eaten by dogs, and the donkey was laughing at all the blows and sores with that fleshless mouth which was nothing but teeth. And it would have been better if it had never been born.

The lava waste stretched out, melancholy and bare, as far as the eye could see, and rose into peaks and fell into ravines, black and wrinkled, with not a cricket to chirp on it and not a bird to fly over it. Nothing could be heard, not even the pickaxe blows of those working underground. And Foxfur kept on saying that underneath it was all hollowed out in galleries, everywhere, towards the mountain and towards the valley, so that once a miner had gone in there with black hair, and had come out with white hair, and another, whose torch had gone out, had cried out for help in vain, for no one could hear him. He was the only one who could hear his own shouts, said the boy, and at this thought, although he had a heart harder than the lava waste itself, he shuddered.

'The boss often sends me off a long way, where the others are afraid to go. But I am Foxfur, and if I don't come back, no one will look for me.'

And yet, on fine summer nights the stars shone brightly even on the lava waste, and the countryside round about was itself black, like the lava waste, but Foxfur, tired from the long day's work, stretched out on his palliasse with his face turned up to the sky, to enjoy that peace and those illuminations up above. And so he hated moonlit nights, when the sea was swarming with sparkling lights, and the countryside could be seen outlined vaguely here and there. The lava waste seemed then more bare and desolate. 'For us who are made to live underground,' thought Foxfur, 'it ought to be dark always and everywhere.' A screech owl would hoot above the lava waste and flutter about here and there. Then Foxfur thought, 'Even that owl can sense that there are dead people under the ground here, and it's desperate because it can't go and find them.'

Frog was afraid of the owls and the bats, but Foxfur told him off, because anyone who has to live alone must be afraid of nothing, and even the grey donkey was not afraid of the dogs which tore its flesh off, now that its flesh no longer felt it painful to be eaten.

'You were used to working on roofs like a cat,' he said to him, 'and that was quite different. Now that you've got to live underground, like the rats, you mustn't be afraid of rats any more, or of bats, which are only old rats with wings, and rats like living in the company of the dead.'

Frog, on the other hand, took some pleasure in explaining to him what the stars were doing up there above. And he told him that up there was Paradise, where dead people go when they have been good and not annoyed their parents. 'Who told you that?' asked Foxfur, and Frog said that his mother had told him.

Well then, Foxfur scratched his head, smiled, and gave him the opinion of a malicious little brat who knows what's what. 'Your mother says that to you because you shouldn't wear breeches but a skirt.'

And after he had thought about it a while:

'My father was a good man and harmed nobody, and so they called him Jackass. And yet he's down there, and they've even found his tools and shoes and these breeches here which I'm wearing.'

Shortly afterwards Frog, who had been ailing for some time, fell so ill that they had to carry him out of the pit that evening on a donkey, stretched between the baskets, shivering with fever like a frightened rabbit. One workman said that that boy would never have made old bones doing that job, and that to work in a mine without losing your life you had to be born to it. Then Foxfur felt proud of being born to it and keeping so healthy and strong in that unhealthy atmosphere, and with all those hardships. He took the burden of Frog on himself, and cheered him up in his own way, shouting at him and hitting him. But on one occasion, when he was hitting him on the back, Frog threw up a lot of blood. Then Foxfur was frightened to death, and he looked into Frog's nose and mouth to see what he had done to him, and swore that he could not have done him much harm, beating him as he did. And to demonstrate this to him, he hit himself hard on his chest and back with a stone. In fact, a workman who happened to be there gave him a great kick on his shoulders, a kick which echoed like a drum, and yet Foxfur did not move, and only when the workman had gone away did he add, 'You see that? He's done nothing to me. And he hit me much harder than I hit you. I swear he did.'

Meanwhile Frog did not get any better, and he went on feverishly spitting blood every day. Then Foxfur did steal a little of his week's pay to buy Frog some wine and hot soup, and he gave him his almost-new breeches to keep him better covered. But Frog was coughing all the time and he seemed at times to be suffocating, and in the evenings there was no way to stop him shivering with the fever, neither with sacks nor by covering him with straw, nor by placing him in front of a blaze. Foxfur stood there silent and motionless, bending over him with his hands on his knees, fixing him with those nasty, wide-open eyes, as if he wished to paint his portrait. And then when he heard him give a feeble moan, and saw his worn-out face and his dull eyes, just like the dead donkey panting in exhaustion under its load as it climbed up the track from the pit, he muttered to him, 'It's better if you croak quickly! If you've got to suffer like that, it's better to croak!' And the boss said that Foxfur was quite capable of smashing the boy's head in, and they had better keep an eye on him.

At long last one Monday Frog failed to come to the pit, and the boss washed his hands of him, because in the state he was reduced to by now he was more of a nuisance than anything. Foxfur found out where he lived, and on the Saturday he went to see him. Poor Frog already belonged more to the other world than to this one, and his mother wept in her desperation just as if her son were one of those who earn ten lire a week.

This was something which Foxfur just could not under-stand, and he asked Frog why his mother was shrieking like that, when for two months he had not even earned as much as he ate. But poor Frog paid no attention to him, and seemed to be only concerned with counting the beams in the ceiling. Then the redhead racked his brains and decided that Frog's mother was shrieking in that way because her little son had always been weak and sickly, and she had always looked after him like one of those brats who are never weaned. He himself, on the contrary, had been healthy and strong, and a redhead, and his mother had never wept for him because she had never been afraid of losing him.

Shortly afterwards they said in the pit that Frog was dead, and Foxfur thought that now the owl was hooting for him too in the night, and he went back to see the bare bones of the grey donkey, in the ravine where he used to go with Frog. Now there was nothing left of the grey donkey but bones here and there, and Frog too would be like that, and his mother would dry her eyes, because Foxfur's mother had dried hers after Misciu's death, and now she had married again and gone to live at Cifali, and his sister had married too, and the house was shut up. From now on, when he was beaten it would not matter to them any more, and it would not matter even to him, and when he was like the grey donkey or Frog he would not feel anything any more.

Round about that time a man came to work in the pit who had never been seen before, and who kept himself hidden as much as he could. The other workmen said among themselves that he had escaped from prison, and that if he was caught he would be shut up again for years and years. It was then that Foxfur learnt that prison was a place where they put thieves and bad lots like himself, and shut them up for ever, and kept an eye on them.

From that time he felt an unhealthy curiosity about that man who had known what it was like to be in prison and had escaped. After a few weeks, however, the fugitive said loud and clear that he was sick of that miserable existence, living like a mole, and he'd rather spend his life in prison, because prison was a paradise in comparison, and he'd rather go back there on his own two feet. 'Then why don't all the men who work in the pit get themselves put in prison?' asked Foxfur. 'Because they're not redheads like you!' answered the lame man. 'But don't worry, you'll go there, and you'll leave your bones there.'

Instead, Foxfur left his bones in the pit, like his father, but in a different way. There came a time when they had to explore a passage which they thought communicated with the big shaft to the left, towards the valley, and if that was true, they would save a good half of the labour needed to dig the sand out. But if it was not true, there was the danger of getting lost and never returning. And so no one who was the father of a family would venture on it, or let any of his flesh and blood run such a risk for all the gold in the world.

But Foxfur did not have anyone who would take all the gold in the world for his skin, even if his skin had been worth all the gold in the world. His mother had married again and gone to live at Cifali, and his sister was married too. The door of his home was shut, and he had nothing but his father's shoes hanging on the nail. That is why they always entrusted the most dangerous jobs to him, and the most hazardous undertakings, and if he did not look after himself at all, the others certainly did not look after him. When they sent him on that journey of exploration, he remembered the miner who had got lost, years and years before, and who still walks and walks in the dark, crying for help, without anyone being able to hear him. But Foxfur said nothing. What good would it have done anyway? He took his father's tools, the pickaxe, the mattock, the lantern, the sack of bread, and the flask of wine, and went away. Nothing more was ever heard of him.

So even Foxfur's bones were lost, and the boys in the pit lower their voices when they speak about him in the workings, for they are afraid of seeing him appear in front of them, with his red hair and his nasty grey eyes.

Rustic Honour

When Turiddu Macca, old Nunzia's son, came home from soldiering, he strutted about the village square every Sunday in his *bersagliere* uniform, with the red cap which looked like a fortune-teller's when she sets up her stall with her cage of canaries. The girls, going to Mass with their noses well hidden in their mantillas, could not take their eyes off him, and the lads buzzed round him like flies. And he had brought back with him a pipe with its bowl carved in a lifelike representation of the king on horseback, and he struck matches on the seat of his trousers, raising his leg as he did so, as though about to give someone a kick. But, despite all this, Lola, the daughter of Farmer Angelo, had not shown herself either at Mass or on her balcony, because she had got engaged to someone from Licodia, a carter who had four Sortino mules in his stable. As soon as Turiddu heard of it, Good God, he'd have his guts out, he'd have the guts out of that fellow from Licodia! But he did not do anything, except let off steam by singing every angry song he knew under that beauty's window.

'Hasn't Nunzia's Turiddu got anything better to do,' asked the neighbours, 'than spend the night in song like a lonely thrush?'

At long last he did come across Lola as she was returning from a pilgrimage to Our Lady of Peril. But when she saw him she did not change colour. It was as though none of this was anything to do with her.

'It's a lucky man who catches sight of you,' he said to her.

'Oh, Turiddu! They told me you'd come back on the first of the month.'

'I was told some other things too,' he replied. 'Is it true that

68

you're marrying Alfio the carter?'

'I am, God willing,' Lola replied, pulling the two corners of her kerchief up to her chin.

'You're doing God's will by chopping and changing as it suits you! And was it the will of God that I should come back home from as far away as I did, just to hear this pleasant news, Lola?'

The wretched man tried to put a brave face on it, but his voice had gone hoarse. And as he walked behind the girl he swayed about, with the tassel of his cap swinging here and there on his shoulders. To be honest, she was sorry to see him with such a long face, but she had not the heart to beguile him with pleasant words.

'Look, Turiddu,' she told him finally, 'you must let me catch up with my friends. What would people say if they saw me with you?'

'You're right,' Turiddu replied. 'Now that you're going to marry Alfio, who has four mules in his stable, we mustn't make people talk. My poor mother, on the other hand, had to sell our bay mule and that bit of a vineyard by the main road, when I was a soldier. The good old days have gone, and you don't remember the times when we used to speak to each other from the window and from the farmyard, and how, before I went away, you gave me that handkerchief! God knows what tears I wept in it as I went away, so far away that even the name of our village was not known where I went. Well, goodbye now, Lola. These things come and go, and now it's all over between us.'

Lola married the carter, and on Sundays she would sit on the balcony, with her hands on her belly in order to let people see all the huge gold rings which her husband had given her. Turiddu continued to walk up and down the little street, with his pipe in his mouth and his hands in his pockets, with an air of indifference, eyeing the girls. But it ate away at him inside to think Lola's husband had all that gold, and that she pretended not to notice him when he walked by. 'I'll give that bitch one in the eye,' he muttered.

Opposite Alfio lived Farmer Cola, who was rolling in money, so they said, and had a daughter still at home. Turiddu worked it so that he was taken on by Farmer Cola, and he began to hang about the house and say sweet nothings to the girl.

'Why don't you go and say these nice things to Lola?' asked Santa.

'Lola is a great lady now. Lola has married a big shot now!'

'I'm not good enough for a big shot.'

'You're worth twenty Lolas, and I know someone who wouldn't look at Lola, nor even the saint she's named after, when you're there. Lola's not fit to untie your shoelaces. She's not.'

'When he couldn't reach the grapes the fox –'

'Said: How sweet you are, my little pip!'

'Hey! Watch your hands, Turiddu!'

'Are you afraid I'll eat you?'

'I'm not afraid of you or your God.'

'Oh yes! We know. Your mother was from Licodia! You're a quarrelsome lot! Oh! I could eat you up with my eyes!'

'Just eat me with your eyes then, and we won't make any crumbs. But in the meantime lift up that bundle for me.'

'For you I'd lift up the whole house, I would!'

To hide her blushes, she took up a log which was to hand and threw it at him, and it was a wonder that she missed him.

'Let's get a move on. We won't tie any twigs into bundles by chattering.'

'If I was rich, I'd look out for a wife like you, Santa.'

'I won't marry a big shot like Lola, but I have a good dowry too, for when the Lord sends me someone.'

'We know that you're rich. We know it.'

'Alright, you know it. Now hurry up. My Dad will be here soon, and I don't want to be found in the yard.'

When he came, her father began by making a face, but the girl pretended not to notice, because the tassel of Turiddu's cap had tickled her fancy, and was still swinging in front of her eyes. When her father put Turiddu out of doors, his daughter opened the window to him, and she remained chattering with him for the whole evening, until everyone about was talking of nothing else.

'I am going mad for you,' said Turiddu, 'and I can't sleep or eat.'

'Rubbish.'

'I wish I was the son of Victor Emmanuel, so that I could marry you!'

'Rubbish.'

'Oh God, I could eat you like a piece of bread!'

'Rubbish.'

'On my honour!'

'Ah! Dear me!'

Every evening Lola listened, hidden behind a pot of basil, and she went hot and cold. One day she called out to Turiddu:

'So this is how it is, Turiddu? Old friends don't say hello to each other any more?'

'What!' sighed Turiddu. 'He's a lucky one who can say hello to you!'

'If you want to say hello to me, you know where I live,' replied Lola.

Turiddu went to say hello to her so often that Santa noticed it, and she shut the window in his face. The neighbours pointed him out with a smile and a nod of the head when the *bersagliere* went by. Lola's husband was away, going round

71

the markets with his mules.

'I'm going to confession on Sunday. I dreamt of black grapes last night,' said Lola.

'Let it go! Let it go!' pleaded Turiddu.

'No, now that Easter's coming, my husband will want to know why I've not been to confession.'

'Ah!' murmured Santa, the daughter of Farmer Cola, waiting on her knees in front of the confessional for her turn, while Lola was laundering her sins. 'Upon my soul, it's not Rome I want to send you to for your penance!'

Alfio came home with his mules, loaded with cash, and he brought his wife a present of a new dress for the feast.

'You're right to bring her presents,' his neighbour Santa said to him, 'since while you've been away your wife has been decorating the house for you!'[7]

Alfio was one of those carters who wear their caps at a rakish slant, and so when he heard his wife spoken of in that way he changed colour as if he had been stabbed. 'By God!' he exclaimed, 'If you've not been right in what you saw, I won't leave you your eyes to weep with, neither you nor the rest of your family!'

'I'm not in the habit of weeping!' answered Santa. 'I didn't weep even when I saw Nunzia's Turiddu with my own eyes going into your wife's house at night.'

'Alright,' Alfio answered. 'Thanks a lot!'

Turiddu, now that the cat was no longer away, did not hang about the little street any more in the daytime, but whiled away his boredom at the inn, with his friends. On Easter Saturday they had a plate of sausages on the table. When Alfio came in, Turiddu knew, just by the way he fixed his eyes on him, what he had come for, and he put his fork down on his plate.

'You want me to do something for you, Alfio?' he asked.

'No, Turiddu. But it's a while since I saw you, and I wanted to speak to you about something which you know about.'

Turiddu had at first offered him his glass, but Alfio pushed it aside with his hand. So Turiddu rose, and said to him:

'Here I am, Alfio.'

The carter threw his arms round his neck.

'If you come to the prickly pears at Canziria tomorrow morning, we'll be able to discuss our business then.'

'Wait for me on the main road at sunrise, and we can go together.'

Then they exchanged the kiss of defiance. Turiddu clenched the carter's ear between his teeth, which was a solemn promise that he would not fail.

His friends had left the sausages, without saying anything, and they accompanied Turiddu home. Poor old Nunzia used to wait up late for him every evening.

'Mother,' Turiddu said to her, 'you remember when I went for a soldier, and you thought I would never come back? Give me a big kiss as you did then, because tomorrow morning I am going a long way away.'

Before dawn he took his flick-knife, which he had hidden under the hay when he was conscripted, and set off for the prickly pears at Canziria.

'Oh, Jesus and Mary! Where are you going in such a rush?' whined Lola in dismay, as her husband was about to go out.

'I'm not going far,' said Alfio, 'but for you it would be better if I never came back.'

In her nightdress, Lola prayed at the foot of the bed and pressed to her lips the rosary which Brother Bernardino had brought back for her from the Holy Land, and said as many Hail Marys as there were beads on it.

After he had walked some time with his companion, who

remained silent and had his cap pulled down over his eyes, Turiddu spoke: 'As God's my witness I know that I'm in the wrong, and I would let myself be killed. But before I came out I saw my old mother who had got up to see me go, pretending that she needed to see to the hens, as if her heart was telling her something. And as God's my witness I'll slaughter you like a dog so that the poor old woman won't have to cry.'

'That's the way it is,' replied Alfio, taking off his waistcoat, 'and we'll both strike hard.'

They were both good men with the knife. Turiddu caught the first blow, and he was quick enough to catch it on his arm. When he returned it, he returned it well and truly, and struck at Alfio's groin.

'Ah, Turiddu! You really do want to kill me!'

'Yes, I told you. Since I saw my old mother in the hen-house I can't get her out of my eyes.'

'Open them wide then, your eyes!' Alfio yelled at him. 'I'm here to give you what you deserve.'

As he crouched on guard, bent double so that he could keep his left hand on his wound, which was hurting him, and practically scraping the ground with his elbow, he snatched up a handful of dust and threw it into his adversary's eyes.

'Ah!' howled Turiddu, blinded. 'It's over!'

He tried to save himself by jumping back in his desperation, but Alfio caught him another blow in the stomach and a third in the throat.

'That's three for you. That's for decorating my house. Now your mother will leave the hens alone.'

Turiddu staggered about for some time among the prickly pears, and then he fell in a heap. The blood gurgled and frothed in his throat, and he could not even utter the words: 'Oh, my mother!'

She-Wolf

She was tall and thin. She had only the firm, strong breasts which dark-haired women have, and she was not even young any more. She was pale, as though she was always suffering from malaria, and in all that pallor she had two large eyes, and fresh red lips that seemed to devour you.

In the village they called her She-Wolf, because she was never satisfied – with anything. Women made the sign of the cross when they saw her go by, alone like a wild bitch, with that rambling, mistrustful movement of a hungry wolf. She bled their sons and husbands white in no time with those red lips of hers, and had them trailing behind her skirt merely by looking at them with those satanic eyes, even if they had just been at the altar of St Agrippina. Fortunately, She-Wolf never went to church – not at Easter, not at Christmas, not to hear Mass, not to make her confession. Father Angiolino of St Mary of Jesus, a true servant of God, had lost his soul because of her.

Maricchia, poor thing, a good, honest girl, wept in secret, because she was She-Wolf's daughter, and no one would ever take her as a wife, although she had some fine things in her bottom drawer, and her own good piece of land, like every other girl in the village.

One day She-Wolf fell in love with a good-looking boy who had just returned from military service and was mowing hay with her in the notary's close. That is, she really fell in love, feeling her flesh burn under the fustian of her bodice, and suffering, as she looked into his eyes, the sort of thirst which people have in the heat of the day in June, out in the open plains. But he went on mowing tranquilly, with his nose in his bundles of hay, and said to her, 'What is wrong, Pina?' In the vast fields, where only the crickets crackled in their flight, when the sun beat down directly overhead, She-Wolf tied up bundle after bundle, and sheaf after sheaf, without ever tiring, without straightening her back for an instant, without putting her lips to her flask, but always at Nanni's heels. He went on mowing and mowing, and now and then he asked her, 'What do you want, Pina?'

One evening, when the men were dozing in the farmyard, tired after the long day's work, and the dogs were whining over the vast, black countryside, she did say to him what she wanted, 'I want *you*! You who are as handsome as the sun, and as sweet as honey. I want you!'

'But I want your daughter, who's young and unmarried,' Nanni replied, laughing.

She-Wolf ran her fingers through her hair and scratched her head, without saying a word, and then went away, and did not reappear in the farmyard. But in October she saw Nanni again, at the time when they were pressing the olives for their oil, because he was working near her house, and the creaking of the press kept her awake all night.

'Take the sack of olives,' she said to her daughter, 'and come with me.'

Nanni was pushing the olives under the millstone with his shovel, and shouting out to the mule to keep going. 'You want to marry my daughter Maricchia?' asked Pina. 'She has her father's goods, and I'll give her my home as well. It'll be enough for me if you leave me a corner in the kitchen where I can lay my palliasse.' 'If that's how it is, we can talk about it at Christmas,' said Nanni. Nanni was all greasy and dirty with the oil and the olives which were put ready to ferment, and Maricchia did not want him at any price. But her mother seized her by the hair, in front of the fireplace, and said to her between her teeth, 'If you don't take him, I'll kill you!'

Then She-Wolf became almost ill, and people went about saying that when the devil gets old he becomes a hermit. She no longer went here and there. She no longer sat in her doorway, with those eyes of one possessed. Her son-in-law, when she looked him in the face with those eyes, started to laugh, and he would take out his scapular of the Madonna and make the sign of the cross with it. Maricchia stayed at home to nurse the children, and her mother went into the fields and worked with the men, weeding, hoeing, looking after the animals, pruning the vines, in the north-east and east winds of January, or in the sirocco in August when the mules let their heads hang drooping down and the men slept face-down in the shelter of the wall on the north side. That hour between the evening and the night, when no good woman ever comes in sight Pina was the only living soul to be seen wandering through the countryside, on the burning stones of the lanes, in the dry stubble of the vast fields which stretched away far into the sultry distance, towards the misty crest of Etna, where the sky was oppressive on the horizon.

'Wake up!' said She-Wolf to Nanni who was sleeping in the ditch by the dusty hedge with his arms round his head. 'Wake up! I've brought you some wine to cool your throat.'

Nanni opened his eyes wide. Half asleep and half awake, he was bewildered to find her standing over him, pale, with her arrogant bosom, and her eyes as black as coal, and he fumbled forwards.

'No! No good woman ever comes in sight between the evening and the night!' sobbed Nanni, hiding his face once more deep down in the dry grass in the ditch, with his hands in his hair. 'Go away! Go away! Don't come to the farmyard any more!'

She did go away, She-Wolf, tying up her superb tresses once more, staring fixedly in front of her at her own footsteps in the hot stubble, with her eyes as black as coal.

But she came back to the farmyard on other occasions, and Nanni said nothing to her. And when she was late in coming, in the hour between evening and night, he went to wait for her at the head of the white, deserted lane, with the sweat running down his forehead. And afterwards he always ran his fingers through his hair, and repeated every time, 'Go away! Go away! Don't come back to the farmyard any more!' Maricchia wept night and day, and she looked her mother in the face with eyes burning with tears and jealousy, like a young she-wolf herself, every time she saw her coming in from the fields, pale and silent. 'Wicked woman!' she said to her. 'A wicked mother!'

'Be quiet!'

'Thief! Thief!'

'Be quiet!'

'I'll go to the sergeant-major of the *carabinieri*, I will!'

'Alright, go!'

And she did go, with her children in her arms, without any fear and without weeping, like a mad woman, because by now she too loved that husband whom she had been forced to accept, greasy and dirty from the olives which had been put ready to ferment.

The sergeant-major sent for Nanni and threatened him with prison and the gallows. Nanni started to sob and tear his hair. He denied nothing, and he did not try to exculpate himself. 'It's a temptation!' he said. 'And it's the temptation of hell!' He threw himself at the sergeant-major's feet, begging him to send him to prison.

'For the love of God, sergeant-major, get me out of this hell!

Have me killed, send me to prison, but don't let me see her ever ever again!'

But She-Wolf said to the sergeant-major, 'No! I kept for myself a little corner in the kitchen to sleep in, when I gave him my house in dowry. The house is mine. I'm not going away.'

Shortly afterwards Nanni had a kick in the chest from a mule, and he was in danger of death. But the parish priest refused to bring him the Sacred Host unless She-Wolf left the house. She-Wolf left, and then her son-in-law too was able to prepare himself for his departure, like a good Christian. He made his confession and received Holy Communion with such signs of repentance and contrition that all the neighbours and busybodies wept by the bed of the dying man. And it would have been better for him if he had died at that time, before the devil came back to tempt him and to pierce his body and soul when he was cured. 'Leave me alone!' he said to She-Wolf. 'For the love of God, leave me alone! I've looked death in the face! Poor Maricchia is simply in despair. Now everyone knows about it! It's better for you and for me if I don't see you again…'

He felt like tearing his eyes out so as not to see She-Wolf's eyes, when they looked into his and made him lose both body and soul. He no longer knew what to do to free himself from her enchantment. He paid for Masses for the souls in Purgatory, and he went to ask the parish priest and the sergeant-major for help. At Easter he went to confession, and he shuffled along, licking the cobbles in front of the church for a distance of six spans as a penance, and then, when She-Wolf came back to tempt him, 'Listen to me!' he said to her. 'Don't come to the farmyard any more. Because if you do, I swear to God I'll kill you!'

'Kill me,' said She-Wolf. 'It doesn't matter to me. But I don't want to live without you.'

When he saw her in the distance, in the middle of the green crops, he stopped hoeing the vines, and went to pull the axe out of the elm tree. She-Wolf saw him coming, pale and wild-eyed, with his axe glittering in the sunlight, and she did not step back one pace, she did not lower her eyes, but continued to walk towards him, with her arms full of bundles of red poppies, and devouring him with her black eyes. 'Ah! Curse your soul!' stammered Nanni.

Bindweed's Lover

My dear Farina,[8] here is something for you – not a story, but a sketch for a story. It does at least have the merit of being very brief and also historical – a human document, as they say nowadays, of some interest to you perhaps, and to all those who study the great book of the heart. I shall repeat it to you just as I heard it on the paths through the fields, in almost the same simple and picturesque words as the people use in telling it, and you certainly will prefer to find yourself face to face with the bare and unadorned fact, without having to look for it between the lines or through the writer's lens. The simple human fact will always provide food for thought. It will always have the virtue of what has actually happened, of the real tears, the fevers, the sensations that have agitated the flesh. The mysterious process by which the passions intertwine, interweave, mature, develop in their underground journey and in their often apparently contradictory comings and goings – all this will for a long time to come constitute the powerful attraction of that psychological phenomenon which is known as the theme of a story, and which modern analysis strives to follow with scientific exactitude. I shall only give you the beginning and the end of the story which I am telling you today, and for you that will suffice, and one day perhaps it will suffice for everyone.

We are those who repeat – but with a different method, more meticulous and more intimate – that artistic process to which we owe so many glorious monuments. We are willing to sacrifice the effect of the catastrophe, of the psychological outcome, glimpsed with an intuition which was almost divine by the great artists of the past, to the necessary and logical development of the story, which thus becomes something less unexpected, less dramatic, but no less fatal. We are more modest, if not more humble, but the psychological truths which we reveal will be no less useful to the art of the future. Will we never reach such perfection in the study of the passions that it will be pointless to proceed with that study of the inner man? Will the knowledge of the human heart, the fruit of these new artistic endeavours, develop the resources of the imagination to such an extent and so generally that the only novels that will be written in the future will be *news items*?

Meanwhile it is my belief that the novel, the most complete and human of all works of art, will triumph when the attraction between all its parts and their cohesion are so perfect that the process of its creation will remain as mysterious as the development of the human passions. Then the harmony of its form will be so perfect, the sincerity of its content so obvious, its style and its *raison d'être* so inevitable, that the hand of the artist will be absolutely invisible, and the novel will bear the stamp of a real happening, and the work of art will seem to have been made by itself, to have matured and arisen spontaneously like a natural occurrence, without keeping any point of contact with its author. It will therefore not preserve in its living shape any stamp of the mind in which it germinated, any trace of the eye which glimpsed it, any hint of the lips which murmured its first words like the Creator's fiat. May it exist for its own sake, simply because it is as it must be and has to be, throbbing with life and yet as immutable as a statue in bronze whose author has had the godlike courage to be eclipsed by and disappear into his immortal work.

It is several years ago now that, down there along the River Simeto, they were hunting a brigand, a certain Bindweed, if I am not mistaken. He was as accursed as the weed which bears his name, and his fearful fame had spread from one end of the province to the other. *Carabinieri*, soldiers, and militiamen on horseback had pursued him for two months, without ever managing to get their claws into him. He was alone, but he was worth ten men, and this evil weed was threatening to take root. In addition, harvest-time was approaching, the hay was already spread out in the fields, the ears of wheat were nodding and inviting the reapers who already had their sickles in their hands, and yet no farmer dared to poke his nose above his own hedges, for fear of encountering Bindweed stretched out in the furrows with his carbine between his legs, ready to blow the head off the first man who came to see what he was doing. And so everyone was complaining. Then the prefect called together all the officers from police headquarters, from the *carabinieri*, and the armed police, and said a few short words which were enough to make them prick up their ears. The next day it was like an earthquake everywhere. There were patrols, squads of armed men, and lookout men in every ditch and behind every low wall. They drove him before them like a savage beast through the whole province, by day, by night, on horseback, by telegraph. Bindweed slipped between their fingers, and responded with rifle shots when they were too close on his heels. In the fields, in the villages, in the farms, under the inn signs, in the meeting-places, they spoke of nothing but him, of Bindweed, of that relentless pursuit, that desperate flight. The horses of the *carabinieri* sank down, utterly worn out, all the stables were full of exhausted militiamen who had thrown themselves down there, and the patrols were asleep on their feet. Only Bindweed, he alone, was never tired, never slept, always fled, clambered over precipices, slipped through the grain, ran on all fours through the thick clumps of prickly pears, slunk away like a wolf along the dried beds of the streams. The main topic of conversation, when people were in little groups, on doorsteps in the village, was the devouring thirst which the fugitive must be suffering from, on that immense, dried up plain, under the June sun. Idlers opened their eyes wide at the very thought.

Peppa, one of the most beautiful girls in Licodia, was at that time about to marry Finu, 'Tallow Candle', who owned land and had a bay mule in his stable, and was a tall young fellow, as bright as the sunlight, who carried the banner of St Margaret without bending his body, as upright as a pillar.

Peppa's mother used to weep with joy at her daughter's good luck, and spent her time going through the bride's trousseau in its chest, 'all white things in sets of four', fit for a queen, and Peppa had as much gold in her ears as St Margaret, and they were going to get married on St Margaret's day, which fell in June, after the hay harvest. Every evening when Tallow Candle came in from the fields, he left his mule outside Peppa's door, and came in to tell her that the crops were marvellous, if Bindweed did not set fire to them, and that the wicker basket opposite the bed would not contain all the grain from this harvest, and that it seemed to him like a thousand years before he could take his bride home on the back of his bay mule. But one fine day Peppa said to him, 'Forget your mule. I'm not going to get married.' Poor Tallow Candle was astounded, and the old woman began to tear her hair when she heard that her daughter was refusing the best match in the village. 'I love Bindweed,' the girl said to her, 'and I don't want to marry anyone but him!'

'Ah!' screamed the mother, as she ran through the house with her grey hair streaming in the wind, so that she looked like a witch. 'Ah, that demon has even got in here and bewitched my daughter!'

'No!' replied Peppa, with her staring eyes as hard as steel. 'No, he's not been here.'

'Where did you see him then?'

'I've not seen him. I've heard people talk about him. But listen to me! I feel him here inside me, burning me!'

In the village the matter gave rise to some talk, even though they tried to keep it dark. The women who had envied Peppa the fruitful fields, the bay mule, and the fine young man who carried the banner of St Margaret without bending his back, went around telling all sorts of nasty tales – that Bindweed visited her in the kitchen at night, and that they had seen him hidden under the bed. Peppa's poor mother had lit a lamp for the souls in Purgatory, and even the parish priest had come to the house to touch Peppa's heart with his stole and drive out that devil Bindweed who had taken possession of it. She however went on to say that she did not know the fellow even by sight, but she saw him in her nightly dreams, and in the morning she got up with her lips parched as if she too had experienced all the thirst which he must be suffering.

Then the old woman shut her up in the house, so that she would hear no more talk of Bindweed, and she covered up all the cracks in the door with pictures of saints. Behind the holy pictures Peppa listened to what they were saying in the street, and she kept changing colour, as if the devil were blowing all hell into her face.

Eventually she heard them say that Bindweed had been run to earth in the prickly pears at Palagonia. 'They've been firing for two hours!' they said. 'There's one *carabiniere* dead, and more than three militiamen wounded. But they've fired such a hail of bullets at him this time that they've found a pool of blood where he's been.'

Then Peppa made the sign of the cross at the old woman's

bedside, and escaped through the window.

Bindweed was among the prickly pears at Palagonia, for they had not been able to root him out from the undergrowth there, which was swarming with rabbits. There he was – ragged, covered with blood, pale from two days of hunger, burning with fever, with his carbine still levelled. When he saw her coming, resolutely, through the bushes of prickly pears, in the first light of dawn, he wondered for a moment whether he should open fire. 'What do you want?' he asked. 'What have you come here for?'

'I've come to be with you,' she said to him, looking at him fixedly. 'You are Bindweed?'

'Yes, I am Bindweed. If you've come to get the reward money, you've made a big mistake.'

'No, I've come to be with you!' she answered.

'Go away!' he said. 'You can't stay here with me, and I don't want anyone with me! If you've come looking for money, you've made a big mistake, I tell you. I've nothing. Look! For two days I haven't even had a piece of bread.'

'I can't go home any more now,' she said. 'The road's full of soldiers.'

'Go away! What's it matter to me? Everyone has to save his own skin!'

She was just turning her back, like a dog that has been driven away by kicks, when Bindweed called out, 'Look, go and fetch me a flask of water, from the stream over there. If you want to stay with me, then you'll have to risk your skin.'

Peppa went off without saying anything, and when Bindweed heard the rifle shots he gave a vicious laugh, and said to himself, 'That was meant for me!' But when he saw her reappear shortly afterwards, with the flask under her arm, well, first he threw himself at her to snatch the flask, and then when he had drunk so much that he was almost out of breath, he asked her, 'You escaped then? How did you manage that?'

'The soldiers were on the other bank, and there were thick bushes on this side.'

'But they've pierced your skin. Are you bleeding under your clothes?'

'Yes.'

'Where are you hit?'

'In the shoulder.'

'That doesn't matter. You can walk.'

And so he let her stay with him. She followed him, with her clothes all torn, running a temperature with her wound, and without shoes. She would go to get him a flask of water or a crust of bread, and when she returned empty-handed, through the rifle fire, her lover, consumed with hunger and thirst, beat her. At last, one night when the moon was shining on the prickly pears, Bindweed said to her, 'They're coming!' And he made her lean back against the rock at the bottom of the hollow, and then fled away. Among the bushes the rifle shots came thicker and faster, and the darkness was lit up here and there with quick flashes. Suddenly Peppa heard a trampling nearby, and she saw Bindweed coming back, dragging a broken leg, and leaning against the trunks of the prickly pears to reload his carbine. 'It's over!' he told her. 'Now they've got me.' And what froze her blood more than anything was the glitter in his eyes, which made him look like a madman. Then when he fell down on the dry branches like a bundle of wood, the militiamen were on top of him in a flash.

The next day they dragged him through the streets of the village, on a cart, all ragged and bloody. The people who crowded to see him started to laugh when they saw how tiny he was, and pale and ugly, just like Mr Punch. And this was the man for whom Peppa had left Finu, Tallow Candle! Poor Tallow Candle went and hid himself away, as if he had something to be ashamed of, and as for Peppa, they led her off between the soldiers, handcuffed, like another thief, she who had as much gold as St Margaret! Peppa's poor mother had to sell 'all the white things' of the trousseau, and the gold earrings, and the rings for her ten fingers, to pay a lawyer to represent her daughter, and then take her back into her home again, poor, sick, disgraced, as ugly now as Bindweed, and with his son in her arms. But when they gave her back to her mother, at the end of the trial, her mother said a Hail Mary, in the bare, dark guardroom, among the *carabinieri*. It seemed to the poor old woman that they were giving her a treasure, for she had nothing else, and she wept like a fountain in sheer relief. Peppa, on the other hand, seemed to have no more tears left to shed, and she said nothing, and no one saw her in the village any more, despite the fact that the two women had to go and earn their bread with their own hands. People said that Peppa had learnt her trade among the prickly pears, and that she went out at night to thieve. The truth was that she stayed in a corner of the kitchen like a wild beast. And she only came out when the old woman died of hard work, and the house had to be sold.

'Look!' said Tallow Candle, who still loved her. 'I could knock your head against the wall because of the harm you've done to yourself and other people.'

'That is true!' replied Peppa. 'I know. It was the will of God.'

When the house was sold, and those odds and ends which she still had, she went away out of the village, by night just as she had returned to it, without looking back at the roof under which she had slept for such a long time. She went away to do the will of God in the city, with her boy, near to the prison in which Bindweed was locked up. She could see nothing but the dismal shutters on the great silent façade, and the sentries drove her away if she stood still to look to see where he might be. At last they told her that he had not been there for some time, that he had been taken away, beyond the sea, handcuffed and with the basket hanging from his neck. She said nothing. She did not move away from the city, because she did not know where to go, and there was no one waiting for her. She earned a miserable living doing jobs for the soldiers and for the warders, as though she herself were part of that great, gloomy, silent building. For the *carabinieri*, since they had captured Bindweed in the thick of the prickly pears and broken his leg with their bullets, she felt a sort of respectful tenderness, a sort of admiration of brute force. On feast-days, when she saw them with their plumes and their gleaming epaulettes, stiff as ramrods in their dress uniforms, she devoured them with her eyes, and she was always about in the barracks, sweeping the big rooms and shining the boots, so that they called her 'the *carabinieri*'s duster'. Only when she saw them fastening their weapons on when night had fallen, and going out in pairs, with their trousers rolled up, their revolvers lying against their stomachs, or when they were mounting their horses, under the street lamp which made their carbines glitter, or when she heard the trample of the horses' feet die away in the darkness, together with the rattle of their sabres, then she always went pale, and she shuddered as she closed the stable door. And when her brat was playing with the other lads on the open space in front of the prison, running between the soldiers' legs, and the other lads were shouting after him, 'Bindweed's boy, Bindweed's boy!' then she lost her temper and chased them off with stones.

The War of the Saints

All of a sudden – while St Rocco was going quietly along the street, under his canopy, with all the dogs on leads, and a large number of candles lit all round, and the band, the procession, and the crowd of devotees – there was a turmoil, a stampede, a rumpus: priests dashing off with their cassocks in the air, and with trumpets and clarinets in their faces, women shrieking, blood flowing in streams, and blows from sticks raining down like overripe pears, right under the nose of the blessed St Rocco. The magistrate, the mayor, the *carabinieri* rushed to the spot. The broken bones were taken to hospital, the worst rioters went to spend the night in gaol, the saint returned to the church (at a run rather than at the slow pace of a procession), and the feast ended up like a Punch and Judy show.

That all came from the envy of those who lived in the parish of St Pascal. That year the devotees of St Rocco had spent an arm and a leg to do things in a big way. The band had come from the city, they had set off more than two thousand fire-crackers, and there was even a new banner, all embroidered with gold, weighing more than a hundred kilograms, so they said, and which in the middle of the crowd looked exactly like 'a foam of gold'. All this must have annoyed the parishioners of St Pascal dreadfully, so that in the end one of them lost all patience and started to howl, turning deathly pale, 'Long live St Pascal!' And that was when the first blows were struck.

Because to go and say 'Long live St Pascal!' right in the face of St Rocco in person is a flagrant provocation. It is like spitting in someone's house, or like someone amusing himself by pinching the woman whom you have on your arm. In such circumstances there are no Christs or devils any more, and you trample underfoot what little respect you do have for other saints (since they are ultimately all related to one another). If you are in church, the benches go flying through the air, in processions bits of candles rain down like bats, and at home soup plates fly around.

'Hell's teeth!' yelled Nino, black and blue all over. 'I'd like to see who's got the guts to shout "long live St Pascal" just once more!'

'That's me!' was the furious reply from Turi, 'the tanner', who was shortly to be Nino's brother-in-law, and was beside himself from a blow which had landed on him in the brawl and which had left him half-blind. 'Long live St Pascal for ever!'

'For the love of God! For the love of God!' screamed Turi's sister Saridda, rushing between her brother and her fiancé, for all three of them had been walking in love and friendship until that very moment.

Nino, the fiancé, was bawling mockingly, 'Long live my boots! Long live St Boot!'

'What the hell!' yelled Turi, with foam round his mouth, and his eye swollen and livid like an aubergine. 'To hell with St Rocco and you and your boots! Take that!'

So they exchanged blows that would have felled an ox, until their friends by dint of blows and kicks managed to separate them. Saridda, who had become angry too, was screaming 'Long live St Pascal', and it would not have taken much for the engaged pair to have started slapping each other, as if they were already man and wife.

On occasions like, this parents and children come to blows, and wives leave their husbands, if someone from the parish of St Pascal has had the misfortune to marry someone from the parish of St Rocco.

'I don't want to hear that fellow's name ever again!' yelled

Saridda, with her hands on her hips, to her neighbours who were asking her why her marriage had gone up in smoke. 'Not even if they give him to me dressed in gold and silver. No!'

'Saridda can rot as far as I'm concerned!' said Nino for his part, while they were at the inn washing his face which was covered in blood. 'They're a bunch of tramps and cowards in that parish of tanners! I must have been sozzled when it came into my head to go and look for a sweetheart there.'

'Since this is the way it is,' concluded the mayor, 'and you can't carry a saint through the square without coming to blows, till it's like a beargarden, I want no more feast-days, no more forty-hour devotions, and if they show me one little candle, I'll send them all to gaol.'

It had all come to this because the diocesan bishop had granted the privilege of wearing the mozzetta to the priests of St Pascal. The parishioners of St Rocco, whose priests did not have the mozzetta, had even gone to Rome to kick up a fuss at the feet of the Holy Father, with their hands full of documents on stamped paper, and all the rest. But it had all been in vain, because their adversaries in the lower parish, whom everybody could remember without any shoes on their feet, had become as rich as lords with the new tanning industry, and we all know that in this world justice is bought and sold like the soul of Judas.

At St Pascal's they were expecting the monsignor's delegate, who was a resolute man, with two silver buckles weighing half a pound each on his shoes (so they said who had seen him), and was coming to bring the mozzetta for the canons. So they, for their part, had brought along the band to go to meet the monsignor's delegate three miles outside the village, and it was said that in the evening there would be fireworks in the square, and the words 'Long live St Pascal' in big letters.

And so the parishioners of St Rocco were in a great ferment, and some of them, the most excited, were stripping the bark off cudgels of pear- and cherrywood, as big as poles, and muttering, 'If there has to be music, then you've got to carry something to beat the time with!'

The bishop's delegate ran a great risk of ending up after his triumphal entry with some broken bones. But the reverend gentleman, who was no fool, left the band waiting for him outside the village, and on foot, by various short cuts, he came quietly to the presbytery, where he called a meeting of the ringleaders of the two parties.

When those fine fellows found themselves face to face, after having been at odds for such a long time, they looked each other straight in the eye, as if they felt a great desire to tear those eyes out, and it took all the authority of the reverend gentleman, who was wearing a new cloth cape for the occasion, to get the ice-cream and the other refreshments served without causing any disturbance.

'This is how it should be!' said the mayor, with his nose buried in a glass. 'When they want me to help make peace, they'll always find me here.'

The delegate said that in fact he had come as a conciliator, bearing an olive branch, like Noah's dove, and he gave them a pep talk and went round distributing smiles and handshakes, and he kept on saying, 'You gentleman must do me the favour of drinking a glass of chocolate with me in the sacristy on the feast-day.'

'Let's leave the feast-day out of it,' said the assistant magistrate, 'or there'll be more trouble.'

'You get trouble when there's all this overbearing behaviour, and a fellow isn't allowed to make his own amusements any more, spending his own money!' exclaimed

Bruno the wheelwright.

'I wash my hands of it. The orders from the government are precise. If you celebrate the feast, I'll send for the *carabinieri*. I want everything in good order.'

'I'll answer for good order!' announced the mayor, beating on the ground with his umbrella and casting his eyes round.

'That's great! As if we didn't know that it's your brother-in-law Bruno who tells you what to think!' the assistant magistrate put in once more.

'And you're putting yourself into opposition out of spite, because you resent that fine for the washing which you just can't stomach!'

'Gentlemen! Gentlemen!' the delegate kept on exhorting them. 'We won't achieve anything by this!'

'We'll have a revolution, we will!' shouted Bruno, with his hands in the air.

Fortunately the parish priest had quickly put the cups and glasses in a safe place, and the sacristan had run off at breakneck speed to dismiss the band which, having learnt of the delegate's arrival, were rushing up to welcome him, blowing their cornets and clarinets.

'We won't achieve anything by this!' grumbled the delegate, annoyed because the harvest was already ripe in his part of the world, while he had to waste his time with Bruno and the assistant magistrate, who were at daggers drawn. 'What's all this business about a fine for washing?'

'The usual bullying. You can't hang a handkerchief out of the window to dry now, without them hitting you with a fine. The wife of the assistant magistrate, relying on her husband's status (there always used to be some respect for authority), used to dry all her week's washing on the terrace, you know... a little thing, for God's sake... But now, with this new law, it's a mortal sin, and even dogs and hens are prohibited, and other animals which, with all due respect, up to now have kept the streets clean. And the first time it rains, it'll only be by the grace of God if we don't all drown in filth. The truth of the matter is that Councillor Bruno has it in for the assistant magistrate for giving a certain decision against him.'

The delegate, to reconcile these people, remained tied to the confessional, roosting like an owl, from morning to evening, and all the women wanted to be confessed by the bishop's representative, who had plenary absolution for every kind of sin, as if he had been the monsignor himself.

'Father!' said Saridda, with her nose pressed against the grille in the confessional. 'Every Sunday Nino makes me sin in church.'

'How, my child?'

'That fellow was going to be my husband, before all this talk in the village, but now that the engagement is broken off, he places himself by the high altar, to look at me and laugh with all his friends right through the Mass.'

And when the reverend tried to touch Nino's heart:

'She's the one who turns her back on me when she sees me, as if I was a beggar,' responded the peasant.

However, he was the one who, if Saridda was crossing over the square on a Sunday, pretended to be deep in conversation with the sergeant-major of the *carabinieri*, or some other big cheese, and not even to notice her. Or else Saridda was much occupied making little lanterns out of coloured paper, and arranging them along the window, right in front of his ugly mug, pretending she was putting them there to dry. On one occasion, when they found themselves together at a baptism, they did not even say hello, as if they had never seen each other before, and in fact Saridda flirted with the baby's godfather.

'Lousy godfather!' sneered Nino. 'Godfather to a girl! When a girl is born even the rafters in the roof break up.'

And Saridda, pretending to be speaking to the new mother:

'It's an ill wind that blows nobody any good. Sometimes, when you think you've lost a treasure, you find that you ought to thank God and St Pascal for it. Because you don't really know anyone until it comes to the crunch.'

Or again:

'You've got to take things as they come, and the worst thing is to get annoyed over things that aren't worth the trouble. When one pope dies, we get another.'

Or again:

'Babies are born just as destiny decides, just like marriages. Because it's better to marry someone who truly loves you, and has no ulterior motive, even if he has nothing, no land, no mules, nothing.'

The drum sounded in the square, the muffled drum. 'The mayor says there'll be a feast-day,' whispered the crowd.

'I'll fight till kingdom come! I'll spend everything I've got till I'm left with nothing but my shirt like the blessed Job. But I will not pay that five-lire fine! Even if I have to leave the lawsuit in my will!'

'Hell's bells! What sort of a feast-day are we going to have if we all die of hunger this year!' exclaimed Nino.

There had not been a drop of rain since March, and the yellow crops, which were crackling like tinder 'were dying of thirst'. However, Bruno the wheelwright said that when St Pascal went in procession it would rain for certain. But what was rain to him, when he was a wheelwright? Or to all the others in his party, who were tanners? In fact they carried St Pascal in procession, to the east and to the west, and they put him on the hill facing the fields to bless them, one sultry day in May, when the sky was overcast. It was one of those days when the peasants tear their hair out when they look at the burnt fields and the ears of corn whose heads droop as if they were dying.

'Blast you, St Pascal!' shouted Nino, spitting into the air and running like a madman through the crops. 'You've ruined me, St Pascal! You've left me nothing but my sickle to cut my throat with!'

In the upper part of the village, St Rocco's parish, there was a desolation, one of those long years when the famine starts in June, and the women stand in the doorways, dishevelled and doing nothing, with staring eyes. When Saridda heard that Nino was selling his mule in the square, to pay the rent for his land which had yielded nothing, she immediately felt her anger cool down, and she sent her brother Turi hotfoot with what little money they had saved up, to help him.

Nino was in one corner of the square, with an abstracted gaze and his hands in his pockets, while they were selling his mule in all its frills and with a new harness.

'I don't need anything,' he replied grimly. 'I've still got these hands, for as long as God pleases! A fine saint St Pascal has turned out to be!'

Turi turned his back on him to avoid trouble, and went away. The truth was that people were exasperated by now, now that they had carried St Pascal in procession to the east and to the west with this marvellous result. The worst of it was that many from St Rocco's parish even had let themselves be persuaded to go in the procession, beating themselves like donkeys, and wearing a crown of thorns, for love of their crops. So now they were venting their feelings in insults, and it had come to the point that the monsignor's delegate had had to clear off, on foot and without a band, just as he had come.

The assistant magistrate, to get his revenge on the wheel-wright, telegraphed that people were excited and public order was threatened. And so one fine day they heard that the militia had arrived in the night, and anyone could go and see them in the stables.

However some people said, 'They've come because of the cholera. Down in the city people are dying like flies.'

The chemist padlocked his shop, and the doctor was the first to flee, so that they could not bash his brains in.

'It won't amount to anything,' said those few who stayed in the village because they had not been able to disperse throughout the countryside. 'Blessed St Rocco will protect his village, and we'll skin the first person we find wandering around at night.'

And even the people in the lower part of the village, St Pascal's parish, had run barefoot into St Rocco's church. However, shortly afterwards the dead began to fall in great numbers like those huge drops of rain that come before a thunderstorm, and they said of one dead man that he was a pig and he had deserved to die since he had stuffed himself with prickly pears, and of another that he had come in from the country after dark. In short, the cholera was well and truly there, despite the guard, and in defiance of St Rocco, and despite the fact that an old woman who lived in the odour of sanctity had dreamed that St Rocco had said to her in person:

'Don't be afraid of the cholera. I'm taking care of it, and I'm not like that good-for-nothing St Pascal.'

Nino and Turi had not seen each other since that affair of the mule. But as soon as the peasant heard that the brother and sister were both ill, he ran to their house, and he found Saridda black and disfigured, at the back of the poor room, by the side of her brother, who was himself recovering but tearing his hair out because he did not know what to do.

'Ah! You lousy St Rocco!' Nino began to wail. 'I didn't expect this. Oh Saridda, don't you know me any more? Nino, you remember Nino?'

Saridda looked at him with eyes so sunken that you needed a lantern to find them, and Nino's eyes were like two fountains. 'Oh, St Rocco!' he said. 'This is an even dirtier trick than St Pascal played on me!'

However, Saridda did get well, and while she was sitting in the doorway, with her head wrapped in a kerchief, and herself as yellow as pure beeswax, she kept on saying to him:

'St Rocco has performed a miracle for me, and you must come too and bring him a candle on his feast-day.'

Nino, with a swelling heart, nodded in agreement. But meanwhile he had fallen sick, and seemed about to die. Then Saridda scratched her face, and said that she wanted to die with him, and that she would cut off her hair and put it in the coffin with him, so that no one would ever look her in the face again while she lived.

'No! No!' responded Nino, looking distraught. 'Your hair will grow again. But I'll be the one who won't look at you again, because I'll be dead.'

'A fine miracle St Rocco's performed for you!' Turi said to him, to give him some comfort.

And when they were both getting better, and warming themselves in the sun with their backs against the wall, and both sulky, they went on throwing St Rocco and St Pascal in each other's faces.

Once Bruno the wheelwright went by, coming in from the countryside now that the cholera was over, and he said:

'We're going to have a great celebration to thank St Pascal for saving us from the cholera. From now on there'll be no more troublemakers and no one to oppose us, now that that assistant magistrate is dead and has left his lawsuit in his will.'

'Oh yes, a celebration for those who've died!' sneered Nino. 'And you, do you think that St Rocco kept you alive?'

'Drop it!' Saridda interrupted. 'Or there'll have to be another bout of cholera to make peace again!'

Crackpot

This is all because we act as though we were at the diorama, when there is a feast-day in the village, and we put our eyes to the window to see, going past one by one, Garibaldi and Victor Emanuel, and now comes 'Crackpot', who is an odd fish too, and cuts a fine figure among all those other madmen who had their brains in their boots, and did everything opposite to what a Christian ought to do, if he wants to eat his bread in peace.

Now, if we must examine the conscience of all those who have had the good taste to get themselves talked about, in the farmyard, at the time for gossiping, after lunch; and if we must do as the steward does on Saturday evenings, when he says to this one, 'What do I owe you for your day's work?' and to that one, 'You, what have you done this week?' – if we have to do all this, then we can't resist giving Crackpot a piece of our mind. What he did was really horrible, and they gave him his nickname because of that nasty business which you know about.[9]

We do know that jealousy is a fault which everyone has, some more than others. And it is the reason why cockerels pull each other's feathers out even before their crests grow, and why mules lash out with their hooves in the stables. But when there is someone who has never had that vice, but has always bowed his head in holy serenity, then St Isidore defend us! we can't understand why he should turn frantic all of a sudden, like a bull in July, and act like a madman, like someone who can't see properly because he has the toothache. After all, those things are exactly like toothache: they give such hell when they're coming as to drive you out of your mind, but

101

afterwards they don't hurt any more, and they help us to chew our food. And he chewed his food so well that he had got a paunch, like a gentleman, and looked like a fat priest. And that is why they called him Crackpot, because his pot was on the fire every day, because his wife Venera kept it going for him, with Don Liborio.

He had wanted to marry Venera by hook or by crook, even though she had nothing but the clothes she stood up in, and his only capital came from his two hands to earn his bread. It was in vain that his mother, poor old thing, kept on saying to him, 'Leave Venera alone. She's not right for you. She wears her cape on the back of her head, and she lets her feet show when she's walking along the road.' Old folk know better than we do, and we ought to listen to them for our own good.

But he couldn't get those little shoes out of his head, or those preying eyes searching for a husband from under that cape. And so he took her without wanting to hear any more about it, and his mother left the home where she had lived for more than thirty years, because mother-in-law and daughter-in-law are like two savage mules at the same manger. The daughter-in-law, with her honeyed tongue and pursed lips, talked and acted in such a way that the poor old grumpy woman had to leave the field clear for her, and go away to die in a hovel. And there was a dispute between husband and wife every time they had to pay the month's rent for the hovel. And when the son arrived at the hovel out of breath, having heard that they had brought the last sacraments to the poor old woman, he could not receive her blessing, or even gather the last words from the mouth of the dying woman, for death had already stuck her lips together, and her face was disfigured, in that corner of the hovel where it was starting to get dark, and only the eyes were alive and seemed as if they had a lot to say. 'Eh?… Eh?…'

He who does not respect his father and mother will bring trouble down on himself and will come to a bad end.

The poor old woman died lamenting the way in which her son's wife had turned out to be such a bad lot. And God had been good to her, letting her leave this world, taking with her to the next world all that she had against her daughter-in-law, knowing how that woman would make her son's heart bleed. As soon as the daughter-in-law became mistress of the house, with the reins loose on her neck, she carried on in such a way that people no longer called her husband by anything but that nickname, and when it came to his ears and he dared to complain to his wife, 'You, do you believe it?' she asked. And he didn't believe it, as happy as a sandboy not to.

He was such a feeble fellow, and up to now had done no harm to anyone. If you had forced him to see it with his own eyes, he would have said that it wasn't true. Perhaps his mother's curse had caused Venera to lose her place in his heart, and he did not think of her any more; or perhaps, because he was away in the country working the whole year round, and only saw her on Saturday evenings, she had become unpleasant and unloving with her husband, and so he had stopped loving her; and when we don't like something any more we think that it can't matter to anyone else, and it doesn't matter to us who has it; whatever – jealousy simply didn't enter his head, and you couldn't have driven it in with a sledgehammer, and he would have gone on for a hundred years fetching the doctor, Don Liborio, whenever his wife sent him.

Don Liborio was his partner too, for they shared a piece of land, they had about thirty sheep in common, they rented pastures together, and Don Liborio gave his word as a guarantor when they went before the notary. Crackpot brought him the first beans, and the first peas, split the wood for his kitchen, and trod his grapes in the winepress. In return, Crackpot lacked for nothing, neither grain in the basket, nor wine in the barrel, nor oil in the jar; his wife, rosy red like an apple, flaunted new shoes and silk kerchiefs; Don Liborio did not charge for his visits; and he had been godfather to one of the babies. In short, they were like one household, and he called Don Liborio 'my friend', and worked hard – you couldn't say anything against Crackpot in that respect – to make the partnership with 'my friend' prosper, and so it had advantages for him, and so they were all happy, since the devil is not always as black as he is painted.

Now it happened that this angelic peace changed and there was the devil and all to pay, suddenly in one single day, in one moment, when the other peasants who worked in the fields were gossiping in the shade in the evening, and they happened to talk about the way he and his wife lived, without realising that Crackpot had thrown himself down to sleep behind the hedge, and no one had seen him, and that's why people say, 'Close the door before you eat, and look around before you speak.'

This time it really seemed that the devil went and prodded Crackpot while he was sleeping, and whispered in his ear all the rude remarks which they were making about him, and drove them home in his head. 'And that billy-goat, that cuckold, Crackpot!' they said, 'who chews away round Don Liborio! And eats and drinks in the mire, and gets as fat as a porker!'

He jumped up as if he had been bitten by a rabid dog, and started off running towards the village. He could not see out of his eyes any more, and even the grass and the stones seemed to him to be as red as blood. On the threshold of his house he saw Don Liborio, who was going away quietly, fanning himself with his straw hat. 'Look here, my friend,' he said to him, 'if I see you in my house just once more, as God's my witness, I'll give you something to think about!'

Don Liborio looked at him hard, as if he were talking double Dutch, and thought he must have lost his head in all that heat, because really you couldn't imagine that Crackpot had suddenly taken it into his head to be jealous, after keeping his eyes shut all that time, and he was the most decent fellow and husband in the world.

'What's wrong with you today?' he asked him.

'What's wrong? If I ever see you in my house again, as God's my witness, I'll give you something to think about!'

Don Liborio shrugged his shoulders and went away laughing. Crackpot, quite beside himself, went inside and repeated to his wife, 'If I see "my friend" here again, as God's my witness, I'll give him something to think about!'

Venera placed her hands on her hips, and began to dress him down and insult him. He persisted in nodding his agreement, with his back against the wall, like an ox troubled by flies, and would not listen to reason. The children shrieked at this strange turn of events. His wife at last took hold of the bar of the door, and drove him out of the house to get shut of him, and told him that she was the mistress in her own house and could do what she pleased.

Crackpot could not work in the fields any more, he had only one thing on his mind, and he had such a fearful expression on his face that he was hardly recognisable. That Saturday evening, before it was dark, he stuck his mattock in the earth, without drawing his pay for the week. His wife, seeing him come home without any money, and also two hours earlier than usual, started to abuse him all over again, and wanted to send him out to buy some pickled anchovies for her, because she had a tickle in her throat. But he would not leave the kitchen, where he sat with the baby on his knees, and the poor little thing didn't dare to move, but just whimpered, because her father's face frightened her. That evening Venera had the devil in her heart, and was really angry, and the black cockerel, perched on the ladder, would not stop clucking, as though some disaster was about to happen.

Don Liborio was in the habit of calling after he had made his round, and before he went to the café to play a game of cards. And that evening Venera said that she wanted him to feel her pulse, because she had felt feverish all day, because of that tickling in her throat. As for Crackpot, he remained silent, and didn't move from his place. But when the doctor's slow tread was heard in the quiet lane, as he came along very deliberately, rather tired from his visits, panting in the heat, and fanning himself with his straw hat, Crackpot went and took the bar with which his wife had driven him out of the house, when she didn't want him, and placed himself behind the door. Unfortunately Venera didn't notice this, because at that moment she had gone into the kitchen to put an armful of wood under the boiling cauldron. As soon as Don Liborio set foot in the room, his partner raised the bar and let it fall on the back of his head with such force that he felled him like an ox, beyond the help of doctor or chemist.

And that was how Crackpot ended up in prison.

1. This is one of several allusions to the characters of Verga's masterpiece
I Malavoglia [*The House by the Medlar Tree*] (1881).

2. This seems to be an allusion to the naval engagement in 1866 off the Dalmatian
island of Lissa.

3. The phrase 'eat the king's bread' is a euphemism for being a prisoner.

4. Onze are old Sicilian coins.

5. The Three Kings are stars in the constellation of Orion.

6. An Italian goats cheese.

7. That is, decorated with a cuckold's horns.

8. Salvatore Farina (1846–1918), a Sardinian novelist and friend of Verga.

9. The nickname 'Crackpot' translates the Sicilian '*Pentolaccia*', which denotes a
man who connives at the infidelity of his wife for the sake of her lover's money.

BIOGRAPHICAL NOTE

Giovanni Verga was born in 1840 in Catania, in Sicily. Initially embarking upon a career in law, Verga soon abandoned this to take up the study of literature, and produced a number of melodramatic novels. However, from 1874, Verga adopted a complete change in style, with works marked by their extreme simplicity and relentless realism. This new technique gave rise to the term *verismo* (from the Italian '*vero*', true), and it is for this that Verga is most famous.

His masterpiece *I Malavoglia* (*The House by the Medlar Tree*) appeared in 1881. In this extraordinary work, one of the greatest novels of the nineteenth century, Verga depicted in remarkable – and almost photographic – detail the lives of Sicilian fisherman. Although he planned that this should be the first of a vast collection in the style of Zola's *Rougon-Macquart*, in fact only one other book in the series was completed, *Mastro Don Gesualdo* (1889). Instead Verga concentrated on short stories, again depicting local peasant life in all its minuscule detail. Most famous among his short stories are 'Rustic Honour' (1880) which was later dramatised as an opera, the libretto being composed by Pietro Mascagni, and 'She-Wolf' (1880). All these short works are characterised by their extreme brutality – both emotional and physical – and by their vivid portrayal of characters.

Shortly after Verga's death in 1922, English novelist D.H. Lawrence published two collections of his own translations of the best of Verga's short stories: *Little Novels of Sicily* (1925) and *Cavalleria rusticana and Other Stories* (1928). To this day, Verga remains chief among the Verist school of writers.

J.G. Nichols is a poet and translator. His published translations include the poems of Guido Gozzano (for which he was awarded the John Florio prize), Gabriele D'Annunzio, Giacomo Leopardi and Petrarch (for which he won the Monselice Prize). He has also translated prose works by Ugo Foscolo, Giovanni Boccaccio, Giacomo Leopardi, Leonardo da Vinci, Luigi Pirandello and Giacomo Casanova, all published by Hesperus Press.

HESPERUS PRESS – 100 PAGES

Hesperus Press, as suggested by the Latin motto, is committed to bringing near what is far – far both in space and time. Works written by the greatest authors, and unjustly neglected or simply little known in the English-speaking world, are made accessible through new translations and a completely fresh editorial approach. Through these short classic works, each around 100 pages in length, the reader will be introduced to the greatest writers from all times and all cultures.

For more information on Hesperus Press, please visit our website: **www.hesperuspress.com**

ET REMOTISSIMA PROPE

SELECTED TITLES FROM HESPERUS PRESS

Gustave Flaubert *Memoirs of a Madman*

Alexander Pope *Scriblerus*

Ugo Foscolo *Last Letters of Jacopo Ortis*

Anton Chekhov *The Story of a Nobody*

Joseph von Eichendorff *Life of a Good-for-nothing*

Mark Twain *The Diary of Adam and Eve*

Giovanni Boccaccio *Life of Dante*

Victor Hugo *The Last Day of a Condemned Man*

Joseph Conrad *Heart of Darkness*

Edgar Allan Poe *Eureka*

Emile Zola *For a Night of Love*

Daniel Defoe *The King of Pirates*

Giacomo Leopardi *Thoughts*

Nikolai Gogol *The Squabble*

Franz Kafka *Metamorphosis*

Herman Melville *The Enchanted Isles*

Leonardo da Vinci *Prophecies*

Charles Baudelaire *On Wine and Hashish*

William Makepeace Thackeray *Rebecca and Rowena*

Wilkie Collins *Who Killed Zebedee?*

Théophile Gautier *The Jinx*

Charles Dickens *The Haunted House*

Luigi Pirandello *Loveless Love*

Fyodor Dostoevsky *Poor People*

E.T.A. Hoffmann *Mademoiselle de Scudéri*

Henry James *In the Cage*

Francis Petrarch *My Secret Book*

André Gide *Theseus*

D.H. Lawrence *The Fox*

Percy Bysshe Shelley *Zastrozzi*